Florida Crossing
a Jose Castillo mystery

Jorge E. Goyanes

JORGE GOYANES

ISBN: Florida Crossing, a Jose Castillo mystery
979-8-218-49108-6
Publisher: Jorge E. Goyanes

ACKNOWLEDGEMENTS

First and foremost; Kathy Williams-Goyanes, my muse, Missus and soundingboard who keeps me on the straight and narrow who initially planted the seed to get me started on this interesting journey. My number one daughter, Ily Goyanes, a pretty damm good writer herself, editor and provocateur.

Natacha Goyanes-Gonzalez; my Big Sis who was always there for family with a helping hand. Joyce Boucaraa of Joy Editing for doing a great job. Subrata Das; for understanding my vision for the cover art and making it happen.

Judy Easton; my editor at The Lake Worth Herald for gently reminding me to write my column for them when I get sidetracked.

CHAPTER1

I was restoring a 1967 Plymouth GTX that had been featured in the television show *Miami Vice*. It is owned by a financial advisor, who lives in Boca Raton. My phone rang with a number I was familiar with Glen West, Senior Prosecutor for the State attorney's office in Palm Beach County.

I touched the earpiece on my Bluetooth, which I use only when I am working on a vehicle. That way, I do not have to put a tool down, and grab the phone.

"Hey, Keemosabe. What's up in the rich part of South Florida? A maid got caught stealing silverware. A rich uncle got caught with his hands up an Au Pair's dress. Or, a rich dowager banged her gardener, and now he is blackmailing her?"

"None of the above, my Cuban brother. I actually need a favor from you that you will like: my office is playing in a charity golf tournament in three weeks, and one of the guys on my team is going to have to go out of town for a deposition, and I need a fourth to fill in."

"Oh! So, now you need me to fill in, eh? Talk about charity."

"Jose, don't bust my chops, you know I had to fill the team with office staff, this is a politically sensitive situation but, since he can't make it and my office has used your help on occasion, you are technically on staff."

"Politically sensitive at golf tournament, are you serious? I know people wheel and deal, and contacts are made, but really?"

"Yes amigo, it's at President McCloud's course in West Palm Beach, and he will probably be attending since he is in town for this event, as well staying at his home Marinlago, which is just a few miles away."

I was speechless, there was no hatred in my mind for anyone, but this person really grated on my nerves with his bombastic rhetoric, outright lies, lack of concern for anyone other than his billionaire cronies, and blatant disregard for decorum, and political correctness.

"You are very silent amigo you don't want to play?"

"No Glen, I just can't stand the guy, but golf is golf, and it's for charity. By the way, what charity is it?"

"Little Smiles, we help kids in tough situations, nurses and caregivers contact us when they have a patient who needs an extra bit of attention, or if they have special requests, say like Make-a-Wish, so we make them come true."

"Sounds good. If it's all about the kids, count me in as long as I don't have to meet, or shake hands with that prick."

"Don't worry Jose, we are just peons compared to some of the heavy hitters, who are going to be there. No one will pay attention to us."

"Okay Primo, count me in, email me the info, see you soon!"

I went back to my project, but little did I know this outing would get me up close and personal with McCloud, and I would have to make some unpleasant choices regarding his safety.

CHAPTER 2

My name is Jose Castillo, I was born in Cuba, but was lucky enough to be sent to America along with my older sister when I was five, specifically in Miami, which has changed much since I was a child. I own Jose's Cruisers, which is a car restoration business that brings classic cars back to life. I also have a one-man private detective agency called *Joe Castle Investigations*. I know the Anglicization of my name is confusing, but more on that later.

My entire operation is housed in a four-story loft, with the garage on the bottom floor, a living room, kitchen and bedroom in ascending order. It overlooks Southwest Eighth Street better known as Calle Ocho, with a nice view of Brickell Bay. I live alone, but my fiancée Kat stays over often, she lives on a beautiful Beneteau Oceanis 54-foot boat that she docks at Coconut Grove marina, which is less than five minutes away. She travels a lot, because she is a fashion photographer, and is involved in photo shoots all over the world, usually at the request of a fashion house, like Dior or Louis Vuitton.

We have been together for a while, and even though the subject of nuptials came up early in our relationship, she shot that down with logic and common sense. She said she wanted to see how she could live with an impulsive hot-headed Cuban first, before she gave way. Those were her words. So far so good, going on five years guess I haven't ticked her off too much, that I know of. I do take inventory of my steak knives if I think I have upset her, though one can never be too sure. Speaking of hot headed, she is an Okie from Muskogee, so on occasion I will get that laser look that would melt steel, but not too often.

The car business pays the bills, and the detective work for the most part is mundane, especially when you are doing surveillance for a divorce attorney, or a personal injury case, where I am hired by an insurance company to prove Joe Customer is not really as hurt as he appears to be, and I try to catch him playing golf, or tennis, or doing contortions while banging his babysitter in the back of the family van.

Once in a while, I do get an interesting case, like the Fansul kidnapping, or in the case of the Tamiami Trail killer, that I fell into by being hired to follow a philandering husband. Sometimes, a reward is icing on the cake.

My best friend is Nate Devine, lead homicide detective for Metro-Dade Police. He was raised in the mean streets of Miami, specifically the projects in Liberty City, even though most of his brethren would wind up dead or in jail, he put himself thru school, and received a basketball scholarship to the University of Florida, got a degree in criminal justice, and worked his way up the ladder at Metro, which is no mean feat considering the politics and favoritism at that department.

He has had me arrested twice for what he called meddling in a case, but I am like a dog with a bone, and if I try to correct a wrong I will, no matter what rules I have to bend or break. Charges were dropped of course after the smoke cleared, and no hard feelings from each other. He was doing his job as I was doing mine. Nate even uses me on occasion, unofficially of course, but if there is something he needs, or wants done and cannot because of his position, he mentions it to me, and most times I will skirt the rules if need be.

CHAPTER 3

For David, it was a tedious job, the planning and surveillance that was involved. He tried to do one every twelve months but, if the opportunity presented itself earlier, he would jump right on it, and it did recently.

He worked as a Service Advisor at a car dealership, so he had access to a customer's address, phone, and more importantly their set of keys for the better part of a day, so that he could make copies of their house keys. He made sure to use one of those automated key making machines, in the local hardware store as to not to bring any attention to himself.

It was a daunting task due to all the planning involved; he could not leave any DNA around for the forensic folks. He loved to play cat and mouse games with the Forensic Technicians. He had gotten much better over the years, and had the system perfected as well as he could, his "kit" consisted of the following:

A bottle of ether to render the subject unconscious; he did not like to refer to them as victims. Zip-ties for the obvious, stun gun if the person had a pet, or the subject struggled. Clear surgical tape to put over their eyes, while he did what he wanted to do to them. Duct tape to tape their mouth shut, which he chuckled at every time he saw a meme about how you can fix anything with duct tape. A supply of condoms, an extra strength Viagra, if he wanted a long session. A bottle of Hibiclens, an anti-microbial antiseptic skin cleanser for cleaning their bodies, a small dustbuster for a final cleanup, a Bowie knife, snip pliers, surgical gloves, leather gloves, a bolt cutter, and two wigs: one blonde, one grey; he would use one to go in, the other one on the way out, in case there was a nosy neighbor.

He had discovered by trial and error that surgical gloves, or any type of tape, were not a good mix because the gloves stick to the tape and rip. His solution was to pre-cut the tape for the eyes and mouth ahead of time, put them on the sleeve of his windbreaker/hoodie, using leather gloves at first, so the tape would not stick.

Once he had subdued his subject, he would switch to surgical gloves, after he was done with them for the "cleanup" which consisted of making them get in the shower and rinse off any DNA from his saliva or touch. He loved running his hands all over them, licking them all over to get their "taste," which was what really got him excited. To him, every woman exuded a different smell and taste, it was like fine perfume to him.

He had taken to shaving as much of his body hair as possible, and he found a masseuse that would come to his house, and for an extra fee would get shaved by her in places he could not get to. He had no mustache or beard, and the only place he had hair was his eyebrows, which he would cover with the clear surgical tape, so not even one wisp of hair would stay behind.

Once he got them showered after he raped them, he would tie them to the bed again, and would give them another dose of ether to knock them out, then he would hold their nose shut, and cover their mouth, until they stop breathing. He thought this was as humane as he could be after all, he didn't think he was a monster.

With practice, he had learned to only target single women who rented or owned an apartment or condominium. He thought correctly that they normally would not have a burglar alarm, like a house owner would. Once he picked a candidate, he would follow her to and from work a handful of times to make sure there was not a live-in or visiting male friend. Since he worked at a dealership, he had many cars to choose from for his surveillance.

He had killed two women in the last the six months, and as recently as three months ago, but one candidate showed up last week that made his cold heart skip more than a few beats, so he decided this one must be done.

She had dropped off her sports car for service, and she was "one of those" as he would say. She was the type to get her way, because of the way she flaunted her beauty, which was considerable.

She slid out of her car and her long legs ran on forever; all the way up to her small waist, leading up to a massive chest, and a classic Mediterranean face. Long dark hair in a ponytail, light grey eyes, and a full pouty mouth. She carried herself with that regal swagger, which most uber confident women seemed to have.

He took all her information, being careful to stay behind the service podium, hoping she would not notice his erection. She was a bit flirtatious, more out of habit than anything. Even though he was not a bad looking guy, she was the type that wouldn't give anyone the time of day, unless they wore a twenty-thousand-dollar Rolex, drove a fancy car, and oozed money.

He made a copy of her personal information after she left. Her name was Monica Tyson, a stockbroker, and showed no wedding ring. He knew he would be scouting her soon, and he could not wait to start fantasizing what he would be doing with her.

David was single, had no immediate family, owned no pets, and his only hobby was stalking and killing, which he had devoted the last ten years of his life to.

CHAPTER 4

I finished up on the GTX, and while washing my hands, I heard the door chime going off. I hurried to my office, looked at my monitor showing the camera angles of my security system. There was a mass of muscled bodies at my door, with a funny looking character at the center of it all. I had no appointments, no messages on my voicemail, so this was unexpected. I stayed in my Jose's Cruisers tee shirt and took my time getting to the door. I had installed a slide on my front door, like they had on the speakeasy's back during prohibition, so I could just open that and get rid of salesmen, Jehovah's Witnesses and the like, without opening the door. I did not know who this group was, so I figured I would turn on the Castillo charm.

I slid it open and said "Thanks kids! But I gave at Boys Town already." with my best smile.

The man in front of me looked like a cross between Billy Idol and Sting. He was about five foot eight, slim, blonde hair propped with gel straight up, like he had been electrocuted. I swore he had mascara on and was wearing a blue velvet suit with a yellow shirt, and matching hankie in the jacket pocket, with a red cravat. He had blue eyes, and his skin was as white as a ghost.

He looked amused and perturbed at the same time. I sized him up as someone used to getting his way based on the entourage that was with him, and the three vehicles it took to bring them to my place: two Hummers, and a new Mercedes Benz AMG G 63 SUV, which with all the add-ons it had it was worth at least two hundred and fifty thousand smackers.

He held up his hand, and calmly said: "My name is Alexander Pushkin, I am here to offer an olive branch from our friends on Miami Beach, regarding the Volkov matter."

I could not resist. "Oh, thank God! I thought you were from the Men's Warehouse doing house calls on your Palm Beach line of clothing. What colors!"

He had an involuntary jerk, I knew I was already getting under his skin, and he was not used to someone not taking him seriously.

He stroked his chin, like he was buying time, and smiled. "Mister Castillo, I was warned about your sarcastic sense of humor, I am taken aback with it, but nevertheless let us start off on the right foot, as you say in America, and let us in, so we may put our cards on the table."

"Cards on the table as we also say in America. You studied us before you came over, or watched a lot of movies?"

"Mister Castillo, I do happen to have a fondness for American movies, but it is hot out here, and I would like to come in."

"Well, do not wear velvet in South Florida, unless your party is in a meat cooler. Come on in, one goon allowed only."

"I must have my security detail with me at all times, you must understand."

"You understand that you are safer in here with me than you are with four of your bodyguards. One goon, or you stay out there and melt, and I'll pass out ice pops from my freezer to keep your guys from passing out."

He whipped his body around and started talking in Russian; three of his bodyguards went back to the Hummers, and immediately started them up no doubt to crank up the air conditioners. It was your typical Miami heat, the type of day that humidity stuck to your clothes, like Saran Wrap.

"Okay, Mister Castillo, as you wish." He said, with a little bow.

"Call me Joe, or Jose if you like, mi casa es su casa." I said, as I opened the door with a little bow, and waved them in, when in Rome...

CHAPTER 5

I ushered them into my office, pointed at the two chairs in front of my desk. "Gentlemen, please feel free to take a cool drink from my vending machine; it has water, soda, and beer."

"No, thank you, we are just fine." Pushkin was settling in the chair, like someone getting ready to give a long speech, or take a long ride. His bodyguard stood by the door, with arms crossed.

"First, please call me Alec. I have come a long way to meet you. I am here as a representative of interested parties that own many businesses in Miami Beach. We studied the Volkov situation, and we want you to know that he was way over his abilities, and his interests were not in conjunction with ours."

I nodded and waved my hand for him to carry on.

"So, our group wants to continue with, as you say, the "status quo"." He actually used his hands to do air quotes.

I could not resist. I did the air quotes myself. "By the "status quo" you mean run your clubs? Buy Mom and Pop businesses out from under them for cents on the dollar? Have escort services staffed with girls from the Ukraine, or God knows where from who were brought here? Thinking they had legitimate jobs, but they have to pay back their fare by prostituting themselves? I could go on, but just want you to know your group is not invisible."

Pushkin was holding his hands together in a praying manner, which I knew from studying body language that he was trying to control his temper.

"Jose, prior to the Volkov unpleasantness, we all got along just fine. We want you to know you do not have to look over your shoulder, and we consider you a valued contact, and might have some work for you in the future." He smiled like a Cheshire cat.

"Okay, Alec, thanks. I will sleep much better tonight knowing this but, sarcasm aside, a few things to take back to your group." I used the air quotes again, I couldn't resist. "I decide what job to take. If I do not like the situation, and I think it is out of line, not only will I not take the job, but I would also turn on you just as fast. Secondly, if someone comes to me with a situation involving anyone in your group, I'll try to reason first. If there is no give on your end, I will do whatever it takes to correct a wrong, whatever it takes as long as it takes. I answer to no one; I have an idea of what is right, and what is wrong, and that is what I use to guide me."

He nodded, trying to look as if he understood. "Thank you, Jose. Your reputation as a dogged advocate for the right way, whatever that is, is well known, as well as your unconventional methods. You do not give up, and you think outside the box, all good qualities. My pleasure to have had this chat." He stood up and stuck his hand out.

I shook his hand and motioned them towards the front door.

I couldn't resist. "Alec, go see my friends at Austin Burke in Miami, they will set you up with some nice suits, which you won't melt in."

His look was not friendly when he said: "I will look them up, soon."

Making friends and influencing people, that's me. I had a feeling I had not seen the last of Pushkin.

CHAPTER 6

Mustafa was finished with his shift at the convenience store. He headed to the rental home that housed five others like him; they came over on student visas, and all worked at different convenience stores throughout Palm Beach County. Two of his roommates were taking classes at a helicopter school, at Palm Beach International airport. Mustafa was also studying at Palm Beach State College, in Lake Worth.

They had been in the States for five years, and had blended in, without arousing any suspicions as their sponsors had suggested; no traffic tickets, low profiles. Once a month, there would be a wire sent from Saudi Arabia to the bank account that Mustafa was responsible for. The amounts were no less than one thousand dollars, and no more than five thousand at a time.

Rent was paid on time in cash; utility bills were paid thru Western Union. They did not belong to a mosque; they worshiped from home further, keeping a low profile. All of them had two burner phones using calling cards, paid in cash. They were instructed that at some point they would be sent on a suicide mission, and they would be considered martyrs for the cause, and their families back home would be looked after.

They have taken their lives for granted after five years, and had assimilated into a country they loathed, and some had actually created relationships and friends outside of their circle, which was frowned upon by their sponsors.

When Mustafa arrived at their home, he noticed everyone's car was there, and including what looked like a rental car. He thought it was strange, because of all their schedules had them out and about at different times, and rarely were they all in the house at the same time.

He walked in and saw his roommates sitting in the living room with a stranger or a visitor. This man had Eurasian features, was about six feet tall, had an athletic build, and had the greenest eyes Mustafa

14

had ever seen. The man stood up, walked up to Mustafa, and embraced him. Mustafa was a bit taken aback, since he did not know this man. There was a large crate on the floor.

The man stood back and spoke with an English accent. "My brother, sorry to intrude in your space, but we have been monitoring you and your group, and we are very proud of the job you have done with your blending in here, in the land of the infidel. You shall call me Aaron. I have introduced myself to your brothers, since I texted them to meet me here. You must have left your cell phone here because you did not respond to me."

Mustafa bowed at the hip. "My apologies, I did forget my phone, and my other one I left charging here. What brings you to our humble home?"

Aaron sat down, placed his hands on his knees. "My brothers, it is time for the eternal sacrifice. I will be here to help you to put a plan in place to strike into the heart of the infidels, who bombed our cities from afar, killed our women and children with impunity, and hid behind the United Nations gutless sanctions. Anyone who does not want to be part of this will be sent back home to continue with their lives, with no ill will from our leaders."

Fadi cleared his throat. "My brother, can we get an exact idea of what we are doing?" He was the youngest of the group and had cultivated friendships thru the flight school he attended, and on occasion went on a date with a customer from the convenience store he worked at.

Aaron leaned back in the chair as he clasped his hands together. "Brother Fadi, I cannot give you specifics, except to say all of you will have a vital job to do, which, if timed correctly, all five of your actions will come together seamlessly to strike at the heart of this country. You are either in or out, and if you are out, I cannot elaborate on the plan. If you are in, there is no turning back, and each of you will receive instructions on projects that, once created, it will be the tip of the spear

15

that will avenge our people. You will have individual projects to do, you will work alone except for two of you, you will not know what your brothers are doing but, if timed right, you will all come together at the same time to wreak havoc upon the infidels."

Fadi nodded, and said: "Count me in brother, I will follow as asked."

Aaron smiled. "Young Fadi, you must be resolute in your actions, no more dating customers, sever all friendships, only the task at hand is the goal."

The look on Fadi's face was of puzzlement. Then, he realized they were being watched. "Oh, I see. I understand, all business, right?"

Malik was next to speak. "When do we start?" He was the other flight school student.

"Very soon, you will receive a greeting card in the mailbox, either left at your place of work, or in your car. The card will have an internet address that is run by us and changed weekly. You will go to that website, use the code in your postcard to retrieve an encrypted message, which will only be up for twenty-four hours. You will then burn that postcard, afterwards. Right now, I will hand out the first of the postcards myself. Please, open that crate, where you will find five bomb vests ready to go, weapons and explosives that are all part of the plan. Aasif and Bahir, you have been very quiet, everything okay?"

Aasif and Bahir were the quiet ones, they kept to themselves both working two jobs, because they did not want to be bored, and did not like American television or movies. They usually read, or listen to music on their I-pods, with what little free time they had.

"I am just looking forward to get on with this plan." said Bahir.

"Me too." Aasif nodded, while gently clapping his hands together.

Mustafa had been quiet, and taking this all in. "Aaron, how do we get a hold of you?"

"Only if it is a dire emergency, shall you text the number that is in the postcard. Text only the number five, and I will call you back, shortly thereafter. Each postcard will have a different phone number in it; I dispose of my burners on a weekly basis. The instructions will be explicit, they might not make any sense individually but, collectively, you will be a force once the plan comes together. Do not discuss your instructions with anyone including yourselves. This has been planned for the last two years, ever since the current President was surprisingly elected."

Mustafa was curious. "So, this has something to do with McCloud. How did you get that crate thru Customs?"

"Thru diplomatic sources with an embassy that is sympathetic to our cause. As far as concerning McCloud, time will tell, from now on if you should have to bring that name up, say number one instead. The intelligence agencies have programs that key on certain words that are typed, texted, and said over the internet. So, I see no reason to bring the name up, understand?" Aaron stood up, indicating the meeting was over.

"Understood." Mustafa walked over, and hugged Aaron. He now felt a kinship, since he assumed what must be transpiring, and the efforts put in so far to get them where they were ready to strike.

Aaron hugged the rest of the men and slapped each of them on the back. "Your families will be proud of you; your names will reverberate as heroes in the cause. Do not open those cards, until this time tomorrow. Mustafa, start withdrawing cash a bit at a time, buy some loadable gift cards, and spread them out between the boys for their projects."

"Will do, boss."

"I am not your boss. I am your brother in arms, be well."

CHAPTER 7

Susan Schliff was the director for the Florida Department of Law Enforcement. She was used to providing security for the Governor and visiting dignitaries, but she had never planned for a sitting President, the logistics were mindboggling, since she had to coordinate with the Secret Service, who were very guarded about their protocols.

She had been warned by her counterpart in Washington that the service rarely listened to local authorities, even though the locals knew their terrain and idiosyncrasies of local traffic and roads, better than out of towners. At the moment, she was in the first meeting between their services trying to explain to Bill Johnson, head of the President's detail, that while on paper everything looked neat and tidy between the Palm Beach International airport, where Air Force One was, Marinlago, the President's summer home and his golf course were all within a five-mile circle of each other. There were a lot of impediments to be taken into account.

They had a map of this area up on the screen, and Susan was starting to point out the things that only a local would know.

"Bill, while on paper it looks like there are three ways to get back to Marinlago, either way you have to go over the Intracoastal Waterway. Going thru Palm Beach is a nightmare, because of the obstacles, like high rises mansions, which are shuttered for the summer, and narrow streets. Coming in from the South, thru Lake Worth, is more of the same. With the added burden of the Lake Worth Bridge being so high up, it represents a juicy target from way too many high rises on both sides of the Intracoastal. Southern Boulevard is the best route, but you have to take into account the I-95 exits, the Congress Avenue crossover, and the airport hotels. So, keep in mind there is only one way in, and one way out of his golf course, and I am sure he will be playing plenty of golf."

Bill Johnson was a Marine veteran from Texas, who commanded a room with his six-foot five-inch frame and booming voice. He still had a crew cut, even though there was more grey than black now.

"Susan, I appreciate your input, but this is not my first rodeo. I have served three Presidents and haven't lost one yet. What is it that you want to add to our detail, keeping in mind our budget has been severely curtailed by Congress?"

"I have the following suggestions, and keep in mind I will use my people, so do not worry about budgets. I have been given carte blanche by Governor Graham to assist you in any way possible. First, let me set up snipers in four buildings: The Palm Beach County jail, which overlooks the President's golf course, and half of the trip heading back to his home, on the island. The next building is the Hilton, on Southern Boulevard and I-95. The motorcade passes within two hundred yards of this place. Third, the South Florida Water Management District headquarters. It's across from where they park Air Force One, and has a sight path towards I-95, and last at Palm Beach Zoo. Even though there are no high buildings, it abuts Southern Boulevard, and there are a lot of trees and hiding places in there." Susan had pointed to all these places on the map.

"Well, Susan, I appreciate it. Since you are using your people, I will accept your help, but they will be under my command, and they will set up on our radio frequency, just like the Highway Patrol boys and girls are doing."

"Great, thanks. Sounds like you are using the Highway Patrol to cover I-95 and its exits. Just deal with me, I have an assistant, but this is squarely on my shoulders."

"I heard you were a tough bird, Sue; you were in the Israeli army, weren't you?

"Yes, I was. But you will find out how tough I am if you call me Sue again. Susan will do, but do not even consider Susie, okay?"

Bill chuckled. "So, I'm guessing that you liked that Johnny Cash song, eh? They were right, you are a tough bird. Glad to have you on board, Susan. We'll get along just fine, do it my way and it will turn out well, got to go now."

Susan felt better, but she still had some unease. She looked at the map again with the new changes, but there was something gnawing at her, like something was missed. She took a picture of the map with her cell phone to study it at a later date. She was going to visit Palm Beach County Sherriff, Rick Broadwater, to run some ideas by him.

CHAPTER 8

The group got together at the same time to open their postcards. They knew they were not supposed to discuss amongst themselves, but they had always known this day would come, and they felt like a team after all these years.

Malik's card said to procure a Palm Beach County Sherriff Aviation department uniform.

Fadi's card said to get a EMT uniform.

Bahir was asked to buy a used van, and park it behind their house for now.

Aasif was asked to buy two used dirt bikes and stash them inside the house.

Mustafa was asked to use the explosive material in the crate, and make six Improvised Explosive Devices, more commonly known as IED's. This was not surprising, since he was the only one in the group to have served in the armed forces and was in the bomb squad clearing roads in Afghanistan. What surprised him was where he was asked to put them. The large size requested of four of them, and how soon he was told they might need to be put in place, which was right away.

The group looked at each other like, what's the big deal? There was no harm in sharing this information.

Mustafa, as the oldest, spoke: "We see that sharing is harmless, but there are smarter people than us involved here. Let us do as they ask, and not share after this. They have good reason and have been planning this for a while."

Fadi spoke up: "Why shouldn't we? Malik is like my brother, what harm is there?"

"Young Fadi, you do not understand. There are many hours of sweat and planning to get us here, we all believe in the same cause. Follow those who are wiser and more experienced, and all will take place as planned."

"I do not agree with all this secrecy within us, we are a team." Fadi stomped his foot, as he said this, and stormed out of the room.

Malik turned to the group. "I will go after him, and calm him down, he is an impetuous young man."

Bahir turned to Mustafa. "Look, I did some research, and number one will be here in three weeks. I can do the math and see where this is leading. I hope Fadi doesn't ruin it for us."

"All will be well, my brother. We are guided by righteousness, and things will fall into place for our success. Let us get something to eat." Mustafa patted Bahir on the shoulder, much like a father to a son.

Aasif did not say anything to the group, but he was worried about the dedication of young Fadi.

CHAPTER 9

Nate had received the news that one of his collars had escaped, while being taken to a hospital. Johnny Norton had been put away by Nate, after a manhunt in the Everglades, when Johnny killed his ex-girlfriend and her boyfriend in cold blood, after he tortured them. Mean as a snake Johnny was, prototypical sadistic type. A history of killing animals, school fights, bar brawls, and unprovoked assaults.

He was a ladies man, good-looking with curly brown hair, and blue eyes. But not too many stayed with him for long, because of his mean sadistic streak. Many of his girlfriends ran away after the discipline got a bit out of hand, when it went from bondage and whips to burning their skin with a cigarette, or a heated wire hanger. There were rumors when he was a teen, that any stray animals around his neighborhood would wind up drowned, set on fire, or hung from tree branches, and Johnny was always the suspect.

Jail personnel told Nate that Johnny hit his head when he slipped in his cell and had to be taken for x-rays. Even though he was taken into the x-ray department by a guard, he managed to sweet talk the x-ray tech to let him use the bathroom, before he was let back into the X-ray area. He escaped from there, and of course the X-ray tech was a woman.

Nate was concerned, because Johnny was a "three strikes and you are out" graduate, which meant that he was in for life after being convicted of three felonies with a handgun. His last arrest was for the murder of the young couple. Johnny had nothing to lose, and he had told various cellmates that if he managed to get out, he was not going to make it back to jail, unless it was in a body bag. Nate prepped his street teams to visit every joint that Johnny frequented locally, to get a bead on his whereabouts, and he would be heading towards Naples to check that out.

Nate finished the usual paperwork, after the meeting with his street team, and headed to Jose's for lunch. He was looking forward to seeing Kat, whom he had not seen in a while.

CHAPTER 10

I was looking forward to having Nate and Kat over for lunch. It was not often I could get the two of them together in the same room, due to Nate's crazy schedule at Metro-Dade homicide, and Kat's globetrotting photography projects.

Creating a charcuterie board, from whatever I had in the fridge, turned out pretty good. It had Serrano ham, Cuban chorizo, machenga cheese, black olives, pimento stuffed olives, Ba-Tampte kosher, sour dill pickles, assorted crackers, and, of course, a loaf of Cuban bread.

For libation, I made some Sangria with cheap red wine, 7-Up, orange juice, a dash of rum, lime flavored seltzer, and threw in a can of low sugar fruit cocktail for good measure. I had the usual beer stock in the fridge of Amstel Light, Red Stripe, and Killian's Red.

The front door entry chimed, and I knew it was either Kat or Nate. They are the only ones who have access to my place, other than Gafford. I knew Gafford was in Miami Beach, attending a Cannabis Conference. He had rolled into town yesterday, so I knew I would not hear from him until tomorrow.

I heard the hum from the electric motor of the elevator I had recently installed in the loft, because my knees were not in the best condition after two surgeries on each, and lugging groceries, and liquor bottles up the stairs was making my knees creak and pop.

When the elevator door opened, it was Kat wearing a pair of cut off shorts, a Florida Panther tank top, flip flops, and the ever-present straw hat. "Hey, beautiful! You are sight for sore eyes." I put my utensils down, wiped my hands on the rag, which was attached to my belt loop, and opened my arms ready for a hug.

"Howdy, macho man, is that a whisk in your pocket? Or are you happy to see me?" The look in her eyes always made me smile, and it reminded me of how much she meant to me.

"Of course, both. I'm very happy to see you, and it's not a whisk, which is a shame, because I had plans to ravish you, but Nate is on the way over for lunch. He heard you would be here and wanted to see you." I gave her my usual bear hug, and she melded right into my chest, which is one of the finest feelings in the world; safe, secure, and "everything is going to be okay" hug.

She looked up and said: "Great to be in your arms again, Papi. How much time before Nate gets here?"

"Oh, darling, He is on the way, so afterwards we can enjoy our company. I have nothing planned, so we can spend time together for as long as we like."

"I would like that, Papi, cause I will be going to my favorite city tomorrow night for a shoot, and I will be gone for a week at least."

"Ah, off to New York again, huh? Don't forget to bring me back some Junior's cheesecake, okay?"

"Sure, like we both could use the extra calories, maybe I'll ship you a pastrami pack from Katz's delicatessen."

"Don't tease me like that, baby, you know what I like."

The front door entry chime went off, and we knew Nate was here. "There's our lunch date, it's nice for you two to see each other, it's been a while."

"Good timing, Papi. Thanks for being so thoughtful." She said, as she blew me a kiss.

We heard the footsteps on the stairs, no elevator for Nate. We did hear his booming voice, "Hey, hey, hey, I saw a BMW outside, so I have a feeling a cute blonde is waiting for me."

She went to wait for him at the top of the stairs. "You bet, studly, hurry your fine black ass up here."

They hugged for what seemed to be minutes. Two of my favorite people, I would take a bullet for either one of them, no hesitation.

I hugged Nate, too. "Hey, brother, use the elevator next time, it cost a pretty penny."

"Shit, bro, I am either at my desk doing paperwork, or sitting in a car at stakeout. I need all the exercises I can get. I gained ten pounds last month." Nate pointed at his gut.

"It's the damn donuts, and that heavily sugared Cuban coffee that does you in, my brother. Come, let's have a healthy lunch for a change, what's your poison?"

"No, it's the damn croquetas and empanadas I get from Versailles, in Little Havana, but I got to watch my girlish figure, so I will take an Amstel Light." Nate took off his ever-present windbreaker, which perplexed me as to why he even wore one in the first place, with the South Florida heat being what it is was to probably to cover his sidepiece, which he carried on a hip holster and the occasions, when he wore a bulletproof vest.

Kat poured two glasses of Sangria for us. I took out plates, and we proceeded to catch up.

I talked about the current restoration project, Kat talked about her upcoming trip, and I mentioned the visit from our Miami Beach friend.

Nate looked up, while preparing a cracker with cheese and ham. "Did Pushkin visit you? Man, that is like royalty in the Vory. You must be special, or you pissed them off again?"

"No, no, it was a friendly visit, more like a feel out process for him. He obviously has enough history on me, but I think he wanted to see for himself."

"Yeah, it felt like a feel out alright, wanted to see if it is true, you are like sandpaper on someone's ass." Kat said.

Nate almost spit out his food. "Now, my lady that is an apt description of Jose, you know him well."

"Sad, but true" she said.

I raised my hands. "I am what I am says me Pappy. What's new over at Metro, my brother?"

"Well, I think we have a serial killer on the loose. I will send you the files, and get your take on it, but, off the record, I have to track down Johnny Norton. Bet you saw on the news where he escaped from the hospital, while faking a head injury. He is a one man crime wave, nasty as they come, mean spirited. Going to start down South in the Redlands, and work my way up the West coast, thru Everglades City, to Naples, then to Sanibel Island, where all his contacts and family members are scattered thru."

"Yes, I saw the news story. They said that he mentioned he would not be taken alive, so be careful, sounds like he has nothing to lose."

Kat put her hand on Nate's arm. "Yes, please do, you know you are family."

"You bet sweetheart, this guy's situation will not end well, thanks." Nate patted her on the head.

"Hey, I will be in Tampa for a few days, let me know if I can do any legwork for you."

"Tampa? What for, Papi?" Kat started to put food on her plate, just enough to feed a bird.

"The Indian Hotel and Casino hired me to do surveillance on one of their pit bosses and a hostess, they want a fresh face, unknown to the area, should be three to five days tops. These jobs are boring, but it pays well, and gets my name out to the West coast of Florida."

Kat had a worried look on her face. "Papi, are you taking Gafford with you?"

"No, baby, just taking Mother with me, should be an easy getaway for a few days, but more than likely I will have my meals at the Colombian Restaurant in Ybor City, while I am there. It's not often I get out to the Tampa area."

Jim Gafford is my go-to guy for computer work, surveillance equipment, state of the art gadgets, and the latest information on the web, and its dark side. He looks like John Lennon, with wire rim glasses, long hair, and wears tie dye hippie clothes, that he is constantly in, even though he is only in his thirties. I bring him along sometimes on a case, when more than one set of eyes is needed. He also has connections with some of the world's best hackers and can get info most government agencies would literally kill for.

The mothership, which we call Mother for short, is my customized Mercedes Benz 3500 Sprinter van; it is a self-sustained operations center. It has bulletproof glass, armored panels, communication pod, with radar, satellite array, a bank of cameras, which shows a 360-degree view of the surroundings, and a Holoportation system that is still being tweaked. It does have some mundane things like a shower, gun safe, a small kitchen, and a hammock for naps.

Even with all the hardware and electronics, it still takes dogged determination, the human element, and sometimes just pure luck to get to the bottom of a mystery.

I started to clean up after lunch. Nate got up, gave Kat a hug, and said: "Primo, if you hear anything in your travels, I am all ears. And don't get your ass in a wringer over Tampa way; I don't have much juice over there like I do here."

"I will try not to, but you know how I am about doing the right thing, no matter who's feathers I ruffle."

Nate pointed at me, with smirk on his face. "You are still tilting at the windmills there, Don Quixote, trying to right all the wrongs in this crazy world. Stay out of trouble, and I'll send you those files tomorrow."

"For sure. Hey, things are looking up, at least I didn't get stuck with the lunch bill as usual, you cheap bastard."

Kat asked Nate: "Hey, dating any Miami Dolphins or Miami Heat cheerleaders?"

"Nah, it's fun dating those beauties, but pillow talk gets a little dicey, my world is full of monsters and killers, and it is a downer to go there. Sure, its great sex, but there's nothing in common after that, those twenty-five-year-olds want to talk about millionaire athletes, or what celebrity hit on them, or what was on TMZ the previous night."

"Oh, you poor man, sorry you are suffering so much." Kat patted him on the head.

"Seriously, Kat, I have to find someone closer to my age, and a bit more mature, who understands a cop's life, the odd hours, the grind, and the frustration with the justice system."

Kat gave Nate a hug. "Be patient, don't settle, look how long it took me to find this knucklehead here."

"Hey, I am standing right here!"

'Thanks for the advice, young lady, will do."

"Alright, off to catch perps and creeps, you kids have fun, and get it while it still works."

"Ha, it still works." I clapped Nate on the back as he was leaving.

"Okay, young lady, time to pay some attention to you, after I clean up."

Kat had that wicked smile that I love to see." Okay, Papi, I'm going to freshen up, and I will see you in bed."

"That's my girl." I snapped the dishtowel in my hand towards her behind.

I was looking forward to our afternoon together, but little did I know what was coming down the pike would keep me from seeing her for a month.

CHAPTER 11

The next morning, as I was getting Mother ready for the Tampa trip. Making sure the fluids were topped off and the air pressure was correct in the tires, checking the propane level for the fridge and mini stove and who shows up, but Gafford.

"Hola, Keemosabe. How are things in J.C. land?" He was in what I call his uniform, cargo shorts, sandals, and a tye-dye print shirt. His hair was in a long ponytail, and he smelled of marihuana, which always made me wonder how he could be so clear and calculating when he was trying to solve a computer problem.

"Not much, Tonto, just was getting Mother ready for a road trip to Tampa, what's up with you?"

"Ah, same ol' stuff, I'm getting my contacts ready for the Cannabis conference next month in California. I am hoping America wakes up and realizes how cannabis could replace current materials with less cost, and less harm to the environment. What's happening in Tampa?"

"Just surveillance for the casino folks, they think one of their pit bosses is playing footsie with one of the poker hostesses." I dropped the hood on the Benz and put my tools away.

"The casino's employee handbook must be tough if they don't want employees fraternizing with each other, isn't that hard to enforce? You know from experience when two people want to get together, nothing will stop the lust train."

"It's a little complicated, Jim. The pit boss is Steve Osceola, and the hostess is none other than Gina Esposito, whose father is Giancarlo Esposito of Little Italy."

Gafford scratched his head and looked puzzled. "I've heard of the Osceola name, they are like big in the casino world, but Esposito? Who is that?"

"He is an old school Italian, importer- exporter of fine goods from New York, always kept clean, but rumors have it that he is the current

31

Capo di tutti capi, or Godfather up there. His daughter applied at the casino under her married name, so they did not catch on until it was too late. They could not find just cause to fire her without creating a shitstorm, they couldn't transfer her, and they also did not want to create any bad blood with her father. Ironically, he controls a lot of the companies that supplies the casino restaurants."

Gafford chuckled. "What do the Indians expect you to do? Get everyone together, hold hands, sing Kumbaya, and get along?"

"I am not sure, amigo. They were very adamant during the Zoom interview, they knew of my reputation for being discreet, and they did not want to use a local, so as to keep things out of the gossip rags. One of the New York tabloids did a story on her, when they found out where she worked, I believe the headline was: "Don's Daughter Daily Grind" and it showed her serving drinks at a poker table. They made it appear that she was a bar waitress, but they didn't show that she was the VIP hostess in the high roller room, and, in tips alone, she was taking home about 10K a month."

"Look at you, mister technology, a Zoom meeting from someone who resisted progress as much as you."

"Hey, I eventually come around you have shown me the advantages of technology. Speaking of which, how is the software patch coming along for the Holoportation program?"

"Funny you should ask, that is what I came to do. But I did not know you were taking Mother on a road trip."

"How much time do you need? I have about an hour's worth of stuff to do before I take off."

"Perfect, a half hour is all I need, I'll get to it, see you in a bit."

I went upstairs to pack and let the boy genius do his thing.

After I finished, and while I was taking my suitcase downstairs to load into Mother, I heard the front doorbell go off. Since I was near my office, I went to the computer to see what the security cameras showed:

It was two well-dressed gentlemen who looked like American Indians, if I ever saw one let alone two.

"Guess they can't wait for you to get to Tampa to meet you, eh, Keemosabe?" Gafford was looking over my shoulder at the screen.

"I recon, so no Keemosabe or Tonto comments for the next few minutes my friend."

I went to the door and opened the peep slide. "Gentlemen, you do not have an appointment, so how can I help you?"

"Mister Castle, if you do not mind seeing us for a few minutes, we wanted to allay some of our concerns before you head to Tampa. I am Sam Jones, and this is my colleague Billy Powell, we are on the Tribal council. We will not be long, sorry for the inconvenience; we did not want to miss you."

Calling me by Castle told me they were not here for a custom restoration on a vehicle, they wanted Joe Castle Investigations. I opened the door and pointed towards my office. "I'll be right in, gentlemen, make yourselves at home, *mi casa es su casa.*"

Gafford told me he was finished with the update, quicker than he thought, but would wait to go over it with me after I would be done with the guests. I told him to run their names, and to use the security footage to run the facial recognition program in Mother on them.

CHAPTER 12

Billy and Sam had made themselves comfortable in the two Herman Miller chairs that I have in front of my desk.

As I walked in, I said: "Gentlemen, I have water, soda, and beer in that vending machine, if you require libation."

"Oh, no, Mister Castle, thank you. We will be as brief as possible." Billy straightened up in the chair and cleared his throat.

"Please, call me Joe or Jose, no formalities here, proceed." I sat at my desk, and turned the monitor towards me, since I knew Gafford would be sending me whatever he discovered about these two.

Sam sat a little bit closer to the edge of the seat with his hands together. "Jose, it has come to our attention that the corporate arm of the casino has hired you to spy on one of our relatives, a Steve Osceola. So, we want you to: number one, be aware of extenuating circumstances, and number two, protecting the family name, reputation, and making sure no laws are broken, so the gambling compact, between the state and our sovereign nation, is not negatively impacted."

I looked at my monitor, saw that Gafford had sent me information on our visitors. William Powell and Sam Jones were legendary Seminole Warriors. They resisted with extreme prejudice the U.S. Government's efforts to cause them to surrender to the white man's plans to put them in reservations centuries ago.

"Gentlemen, unless you two have found the Fountain of Youth, that Ponce De Leon was looking for, Billy Powell and Sam Jones have died, back in the eighteenth century."

Sam sat back in his chair and took a deep breath. "Much like you, Mister Castillo, we Anglicized our names, so we could blend into the white man's world. We are proud of heritage and our given names. Those men were staunch defenders of our culture and heritage."

"Touché, good point, no harm no foul, please continue." They had done their homework on me.

"It is a simple request, I am sure that corporate has the best interest of the casino's reputation, but we are concerned about the family name and reputation also, and we would appreciate you keeping us in the loop with your findings. We can even add some additional fees if you so require."

I pointed at both of them. "If you have done your due diligence on me, you know I will do the job I am hired for, no matter what. And, if there are any laws broken, I will notify the authorities, even if it goes against my client's wishes. Also, I will not be requiring any funds from you; I do not double dip my clients, I will be happy to share information with you on a need to know basis, but it's for me, and only me, to decide who needs to know. I am starting to wonder if this is more than a simple surveillance job, since there seems to be some underlying drama going on."

Billy stood up, and went to the vending machine, took an Amstel, sat back down, cleared his throat before taking a healthy swig, after popping off the cap.

"I don't want to drag you into family, and corporate drama, but there are forces who would like to see no Osceola's on corporate boards for the casino, and ruining our good name would be one way to have their power play succeed."

I stood up, went around my desk arm outstretched. "Gentlemen, I think we are on the same page, I will keep you posted, as I see fit, but I must get going."

Sam shook my hand, Billy did too, but would not let go. He looked at me with a serious look. "Jose, we are very grateful you listened to us, and hope we will talk soon, here is my card with both our numbers should you need our assistance."

I walked them to the door, and met Gafford at the office, took an Amstel out for myself, and breathed a sigh of relief.

"What was that all about?" Gafford took the bottled water from the vending machine. He won't let liquor touch his lips, but he smokes pot like Cheech and Chong on a bender, go figure.

"My man, what is that famous line: it's a mystery wrapped around an enigma? It's not starting out well, and I am not even there yet, but I have a feeling there's more to this than meets the eye."

"Hey, J.C., you need me, I am there. I have a few days I can spare."

"I appreciate that, will keep you in mind if things turn sideways, I hope I can wrap this up in a few days. Next week, I have a golf tournament up in West Palm Beach, and I don't want to miss that."

"Oh my, rubbing elbows with the rich and famous again?"

"I am actually, playing at the President's golf course for charity. I will be okay, as long as I don't have to shake hands with that prick."

"Goodness gracious, please don't get arrested, I'll bail you out if I have to."

"All right, get out of here, I have to go. Be well, and look out for some boxes coming in. Those will be the parts for the GTX I am working on."

I hoped the politics would not ruin the golf game, but, at this time, I did not know how close I would have to get to the President, and have to do the right thing, even though I would detest it.

CHAPTER 13

David was starting to get antsy about doing Monica, he had been doing surveillance on her for a couple of weeks. Between what he observed and the information he received from the tracker, he had put on her car when it was in for service, he had her movements down pat.

Monica was not dating anyone but, on most Saturday nights, she would go to a ritzy Brickell Avenue condominium, and stay overnight. He did not see her walk a dog, so that was checked off in his mind, he had no compunction about killing a human being, but he would never hurt an animal.

She was definitely a workaholic, getting to the office early every day, sometimes a few days a week. Often staying past five o'clock, except on Tuesdays and Thursdays, when she would go to the gym. He was contemplating whether to go into her apartment in the middle of the night, like he had done with the previous subjects, or to do it on her gym night, assuming when she got home, she would shower. He could go in, while she was showering, and surprise her, and that early in the evening he hoped that she would not have chained her front door yet.

He had learned from experience that, once they were going to bed, they would slide on the flimsy door chain, which was really a mental placebo. That really did not keep the chain from being cut with a bolt cutter. The one he had in his kit would cut through that chain like butter, and not make a sound.

He made up his mind to do it next Thursday. Of course, she would miss work on Friday, and unless someone was really worried about her, maybe the alarm wouldn't be raised until Monday, which would be fine with him. The more time that passed before she was discovered, the better for him. Just the thought that it was a few days away gave him a twinge between his legs, he could not wait to savor her taste and smell.

The way he planned things he would stay with his subjects for a long while, usually about three to four hours. He would make sure to leave before daybreak, using the cover of darkness to facilitate his exit. In this case, he wanted to spend a long time with Monica, for him she was a special one.

He had studied serial killers, and felt he had a PHD in their methodology. All of them had kept souvenirs of their victims, which helped to obtain their convictions in some cases. He did not keep any personal belongings, yet he always brought a clean kit, which he would use to wipe their bodies, obtaining their sweat or body perfume, as he called it, putting the cleaning cloth in a Ziploc bag, and later opening it to smell it before putting it in a trash bin that belonged to one of his neighbors, just as a subterfuge to throw the authorities off, if push came to shove.

CHAPTER 14

Nate received a text from the Medical Examiner to come by when he had a chance. He wondered which case this was, wondering which of all the many cases that were under his purview.

Doctor Vishnu Bhomkar was a persnickety M.E. of Indian descent, who had trained and graduated at the top of his class, at John Hopkins University. He always appeared to be rushed and hurried which, based on the number of bodies being sent to him from Law Enforcement in South Florida, was not surprising.

The only time he slowed down, was when he was explaining to the authorities what the cause of death was. He wanted to be absolutely sure they grasped the results, as this would either make, or break their cases. He was short, had a head of unruly hair and a mustache to match, and reminded those who met him of Albert Einstein.

"Hey, Doctor Vinnie Boombatz, how you doin?" Nate said, in his best New York accent.

"You know, Nate, I told myself the next person to call me that I was going to inject them in a vein with air, and watch them expire in front of me, within a minute or so."

"Doc, you know I love you; you are the guy that puts the puzzle together for us, what you got cooking for us?"

"Well, you do remember the young lady, from six months ago, who we figured out was asphyxiated, but we could not figure out how she was subdued?"

"Sure, can't forget her, a real beauty."

"The biological specimens from blood, liver, kidney, bile, and urine detected a large concentration of ether. So, that means that the perp anesthetizes them, which keeps them incapacitated or woozy for lack of a better term. Sorry, it took so long, but labs are way behind in getting results fast."

"Thanks, Doc, that won't help us catch him or her, but it does explain the method and attention to detail."

"Nate, I am not a profiler, but I would say this person is very methodical, a planner who takes his time, and has done this before. I remember doing her autopsy, and not finding any other DNA, except for the victims own and very little at that, which means he spends a lot of time cleaning them and is very thorough."

"Believe it or not, Doc, what that tells me is he or she is probably single, no one to rush home to or to answer to. Thanks for shedding a light on it, much appreciated."

"Just doing my job like a mushroom, they keep me in this dark basement, and keep feeding me society's jetsam and flotsam. Be well, my friend, and go on a diet, you look like you've gained twenty pounds."

"Bite my ass, Doc, its only ten pounds."

"Looks like twenty to me, what do I know?"

"Fuck you, Doc, get an eye exam soon, will ya."

"Love you too. Now, go catch someone for a change."

Nate headed upstairs to see his assistant Buck Taylor; he was going to give him a job he was not going to like.

CHAPTER 15

Buck Taylor was wearing his Pride tee shirt at work, which Nate enjoyed. The cops who were uptight about gays, were always going out of their way to act super macho around him. They were so insecure they had to show how tough they were.

Buck literally ate that up, he had fun calling them sweetheart or darling just to get under their skin, and he was a real pro at doing it.

Nate walked into his office, pointed at Buck to come over.

"How's tricks today, Buck? Aggravating the rank and file, I see."

"Oh, you know, Boss, I can't help riling them up, they are so afraid of showing any emotion, or empathy. They are afraid of turning into Paul Lynde, or Billy Porter. What do you need from me, today?"

"It's a tedious and time consuming job, but if anyone is anal retentive enough for it, no pun intended, you are the one. I am giving you the file on the girl we found at her condo, six months ago. The results from the lab were lacking anything that would give us a new lead, so I want you to go thru her phone records and credit cards, see if there is a speck of anything that we can tie together. See what investigators might have missed. I know it will take a while, and you are stretched thin, but I am grasping at straws here."

"That was the girl who was left as clean as a whistle, I do remember that. As always, Boss, I will do the best I can with the limited resources we have been given, I'll holler if I hit on something."

"You do that. I am heading out, hoping to catch the trail of Johnny Norton, so I could be gone for a few days."

Buck put his hands on Nate's desk. "You be careful, Boss, I have a bad feeling about that guy, bad vibes."

"Don't worry, that guy is coming home in a body bag, one way or another."

Nate had no idea how prophetic that would turn out to be.

CHAPTER 16

Surveillance is boring, tedious, and not what you see on television or in the movies. A lot of the time is spent waiting, and patience is required because, most of the time, not a hell of a lot happens. With today's technology and electronics, there are a lot of ways to kill time, but how many hours of games can you play online?

Thank goodness for my Kindle, and Mother's on-board computer, at least I can read a book check the stock market, play poker, or chess. If not, I would go completely mad.

I had parked Mother half a block away from Gina's condo, and I had a great view of her balcony, and both entrances to her parking lot. Later that evening, after Gina arrived, I would put a tracker on her car to make my job easier.

After waiting a few hours for her to wind down from her job, I went for a walk. I passed by her car, and placed the tracker under her bumper, while it looked like I was tying the laces on my Gdefy sneakers.

I had come in from the opposite side, from where Mother was on purpose, so I could see what was on the other side of the complex. I noticed a gold-colored Ford Expedition, which was familiar to me. I snuck up on it, and slammed my palms against the driver's window, which made the driver jump, and spill some of their soft drink.

Tracy Lewinski, of "At Your Service Detective" agency, lowered the window; shot me a look that could limp a penis. "You, stupid Cuban fuck! What is the matter with you?"

She was one of Miami's most controversial private eyes, she was the first to do television commercials, on the late at night channels. She was the scourge of married men having affairs, and she had a stint on a television show, which caught cheaters.

It was said, that if she knocked on your door, or showed up at a divorce hearing, your best bet was to shut the hell up because she would have the goods on you.

"Fancy meeting you here of all places, you need to get a different vehicle, this tank you drive sticks out like a sore thumb. We wouldn't be following the same people, would we?"

She wiped some soda from her console, moved a mountain of things off the passenger seat, and said: "Get in on the other side, this humidity fucks up my hair."

I settled in, and said: "So, who is going to give in first telling who we are following? Ladies first, of course."

"Spare me the Latino gentlemanly shit, we can flip for it." She grabbed a quarter from the console and flipped it. "Heads or tails, what will it be?"

"Well, of course I prefer heads, you know, like a head job."

"In your dreams, boyo. Besides, you are so far up your girl's ass, you can see what she had for lunch, and word gets around."

"'Tis' true, I am smitten, that is a fact."

She flipped the quarter, and she placed it on the dash. "Tails it is me first." She reached for a vape pen, which was plugged in to a charger.

"So, boyo, Gina Sanchez is her name. She works at the casino, and she is a high stakes poker room hostess, and her uncle, who heads union Local 319, hired me to keep an eye on her. He doesn't like her new beau, and she doesn't trust him."

"Hmm, I guess we better compare notes on all of this, because I have been hired by the powers at the casino to keep an eye on the couple, so something smells rotten in Denmark."

Tracy turned in her seat, squinted her eyes, and gritted her teeth. "Damn Cubano, I guess we better compare notes, I hate getting played."

"So, her real name is Esposito, of the Long Island Esposito's." Tracy's eyes opened up, and her nostrils flared up. "Calm down there, cowgirl, don't go all Loxahatchee redneck on me, I am just the messenger."

"Now, the Esposito's I have heard of who hasn't? They have their hands in everything up and down the East coast, restaurant supplies, linen companies, and garbage service, right?"

I nodded my head. "Yep, that's about right, who is this guy that hired you, by the way?"

"Joe Alessio, of Local 319 here in Tampa, guess if you look deep enough. Now, I am sure I will find a link to Long Island, I wonder what their game is?"

"Not sure what, just yet, but we were both hired by different parties to keep an eye on the same couple, wondering what is up. Okay, let me have your cell number, I'll call you so you can have mine. It's better if we keep in touch, since we are working the same side of the street and should compare notes. I am sure you have a picture of both. Oh, by the way, they told you who the boyfriend is?"

"As a matter of fact, Alessio was vague about it, he just said he had American Indian features, but not to worry, my main job was to keep an eye on Gina to make sure she was okay. I thought it was kinda strange, but the money is good, and they pay a week in advance in cash."

I took a deep breath and told her it was Steve Osceola.

Tracy gripped the steering wheel, until her knuckles turned white. "Son of a bitch! This is turning into a soap opera cluster fuck, what the hell is going on?"

"I'll have my tech guy do a little bit of research, and see what I can find, as far as who all the players are, I promise to keep you posted."

"I appreciate it, Jose, funny to be working with you after all these years. I hear thru the grapevine you are a standup guy who sticks to doing things the right way, but you can be a pain in the ass sometimes."

I chuckled. "Sometimes? Some people would say all the time. By the way, I feel the same way working with the world-famous Tracy Lewinski, I'll need your autograph afterwards."

"There it is, the other thing I heard about you, Jose, that you're full of shit." She slapped her thigh and laughed.

"Think you are funny, huh? I'll be in touch." I let myself out and headed back to Mother.

Once I reached Mother, I sent an email to Gafford, and asked him to get me the lowdown on the board members of the casino, and Local 319. By the "lowdown," I meant a deep dive, other than the usual crap on the internet, to get the skinny on any irregularities that might pop up. I was afraid, in case of the union, it might open up a can of worms, but I wanted to see how long the tentacles reached out.

What I would find out was not from the group I was expecting trouble from.

CHAPTER 17

In the morning, after I started the coffee, I trained one of my CCTV cameras on Gina's front door, so I could monitor any comings and goings. Then I started to read the files on the unsolved murders Nate had sent me. I felt better knowing Tracy was on the other side of the complex, watching too.

I came to a few conclusions about the four cases: the perp had plenty of time to plan his attacks; he was not in a hurry once he entered, which meant he was in complete control of the situation. There were no break-ins, so he had access to their domicile. He had to have some type of contact with the victims, because he seemed to know their habits and schedules. And, all the victims lived in an apartment, or a condominium.

Nate's team had done a good job with the limited resources, and lack of manpower available, due to budget cuts in all of Metro-Dade. They had interviewed maintenance men, delivery dudes, ex, current paramours, and fellow workers with nothing to show for it.

Metro-Dade P.D. did not have the computer hardware Gafford and his associates had. So, I sent the files with the phone records for all the victims to him. I added a note to see if there was a common denominator number associated with all of them, hoping something would jive.

When I finished, I stepped out of Mother to stretch my legs, and walk a little. I noticed that, about half a block away, there were two men sitting in, what was obviously, a rental car across the street from the apartment complex. They could not see me, but I could see their windows were slightly cracked to let the smoke out. I knew it was cigars, because the smell had wafted all the way down my way, a trained investigator I am.

I watched them for about ten minutes, before I called Tracy.

She picked up on the first ring. "Hey, partner, you noticed those two guys in the rental car, about half a block from the complex?"

"Well, J.C., funny you should mention them. I was just getting ready to call you and ask you the same thing."

"Great minds think alike girl. Why don't we go get some breakfast, and if they are still around, we can go check in on them. I will come to you, and we will go in your tank."

"No need to, I checked around, and there is a great breakfast place within walking distance, it has five stars, according to Google."

After breakfast, we walked back, and noticed the men were in the car, and the smoke was still coming out thru the slightly opened windows.

Over breakfast, we discussed if they were still there, we would pay them a visit, so worked out a plan.

We walked up to the car, Tracy on the passenger side, and me on the drivers. We surprised the men to the point where one of them dropped his cigar on his lap, when we simultaneously tapped on the windows.

"What the fuck!" said the man sitting in the driver's seat. He lowered the window and was none too happy.

He looked about sixty-ish, a bit overweight, with a bulbous nose, his skin was white as paste, and had his hair slicked back, and shiny, like he used Vaseline on it.

He tried to open the car door, but I was up against it, not allowing him to do so.

"Can I fucking help you, buddy?" He was getting riled up.

I decided to turn on the Castillo charm. "Now, is that a way to talk to someone who is familiar with local customs? And, who came over to help some visitors with their surveillance?"

"What the fuck you want buddy, waddaya want?"

His accent was so thick, and so New Yorkish, it was not even funny. "Where are you from? Bronx or Brooklyn?" I asked.

"What's it fucking to ya?" He was starting to jerk his leg up and down, with a nervous twitch.

"Come on out, we are just trying to help you acclimate to Florida. We might be in the same business, and I just want to compare notes." I stepped away from the door, and walked over to the passenger side, where Tracy was, and the other man was in the process of stepping out of the car.

They both had bulges under their shirts, and both wearing ankle holsters.

The other man was about six feet tall, wiry, looked like he was in some type of pain, as he moved slowly, getting out of the car.

"My name is J.C., this is Tracy." I nodded at her. "Just a couple of suggestions when you are in Florida, a rental car with two guys in it smoking, and drinking coffee stick out like a sore thumb, you would blend in better if you were drinking iced coffee, and that would help with the heat too. I suggest you rent a van, or a mini motor home next time. Your Hawaiian shirts are too loud, even for Florida, nobody wears fedora hats in Florida, unless you are at South Beach, or a concert. Smoking is bad for you, I thought you guys had a chimney in here, with the smoke wafting out of your windows, and I hope you have permits for your pieces."

"Really, asswipe? Is that why you rousted us? Anything else?" said the driver.

Tracy stepped in front of the driver. "Listen, I was hired to keep an eye on a lady that lives there, and he was hired to keep an eye on her boyfriend." She said, pointing to me. "Is it a coincidence you are out here, too? Bet you were hired for the same thing."

The driver relaxed his shoulders and stance, which told me, according to my knowledge of body language, that he no longer felt threatened. "Okay, got it, my name is Vinnie, and this is Harry. We just got spooked, thought you two were cops."

"Well, we both used to be, but that was another life, now we are just P.I.'s trying to pay the bills, and keep a semblance of order, whenever we can."

"That is funny, we both are ex-cops too, small world."

"Let me guess, NYPD's finest, and both of you had to take early retirement, due to injuries on the job."

Vinnie elbowed Harry. "We got us a real Sherlock Holmes here, Harry, this guy is slicker than owl shit."

Tracy piked in. "It's pretty obvious, boys. By the way, you wouldn't be working for Esposito by any chance, would you?"

Harry twitched and gave Vinnie perplexed look.

Vinnie poked Tracy on the shoulder, while looking at Harry. "My goodness! We have a real Kinsey Millhone here, in addition to Sherlock."

"I see you read mysteries, my friend. I like Sue Grafton, too, when I have the time to read, which is rare."

Tracy looked at me with her palms up, with a "what are you talking about?" look on her face.

"I'll explain later, a mystery series by a great writer."

"Okay, let's compare notes, so that we are on the same page. I was hired by the casino to keep an eye on Osceola, Tracy was hired by Local 319, which is really Esposito, to keep an eye on Gina, and you two were hired by Esposito to do the same thing, and to make sure Tracy was doing her job. Sound about right?"

"Yes, that about sums it up, Paisan. Let's exchange phone numbers, so we can coordinate, and keep tabs on each other, and them lovebirds. I want to get back in the car, and turn the air conditioner on, the humidity is brutal down here." Harry was sweating, like a whore in church.

"Welcome to Florida, boys. By the way, I have a tracker on her car, anything unusual seen by you two?"

"Nope, just the usual handymen, plumbing vans, a/c repairmen, Uber eats, flower deliveries, and the like."

Suddenly, there was an explosion that came from the apartment complex, which made us all jump, so we started running towards the building, as our instincts took over.

When we got to the site of the explosion, my gut told me this was not going to be good, and I was right. It was Gina's apartment, where the explosion had come from.

CHAPTER 18

Nate had headed westbound out of Miami on U.S. Highway 41, which is also called the Tamiami Trail. Not because it was convenient, but because that was the probable route Norton had taken upon his escape, since he was raised and grew up on the Southwest side of Florida.

Nate remembered being taken to visit relatives in Bonita Springs for Thanksgiving as a child, thinking that was the longest trip he ever experienced. Back then, the only way from Miami to the West coast of Florida was on US 41, which was at the time a two lane highway cutting thru Big Cypress Wildlife area, and some Indian reservations and enclaves. The East-West Road between Ft. Lauderdale and Naples, which is called Alligator Alley, was not finished until 1968.

Big Cypress is a nationally protected preserve, so there are no homes or business allowed there. Nate was surprised at how far creeping westbound Miami, Homestead, and Kendall had stretched out closer to the preserve, and how much Naples was creeping eastward in Collier County. He wondered how the cities could upkeep the infrastructure with the amount of people gobbling up houses as soon as they were built.

He stopped at every gas station and convenience mart on the way, showing the clerks a mug shot of Johnny to see if he had stopped in. He made sure to stop at Joanie's Blue Crab café, in Ochopee, to get some catfish, soft shell crab, and collards. Since he was there, he showed the waitresses Johnny's picture, and hit pay dirt.

The waitress, who had a name tag with "Flo" on it, remembered him. "Sure thing, sir, he was very friendly, and was flirting with me, which was funny, considering he mentioned he was going to see his girlfriend up near Sanibel."

Nate perked up. "When was that, miss?"

"Oh, let's see... two days ago."

"Thank you very much." Nate paid the bill, left a big tip, and made a call to his assistant, Buck.

"Hey, Buck, look in Norton's file, and let me know if he had a girlfriend on the West coast somewhere."

"Sure thing, Boss, will call you right back." Buck was fussy about his files; everything colored coordinated with Post-It notes, so he was able to call Nate back within five minutes.

Buck passed on the information. "Okay, Boss, I will text and email the info: his ex-girlfriend works at the Sanibel Island Library, as a librarian, her name is Page Turner, and last known home address is Sanibel."

Nate finally had the lead he was looking for he would talk to Miss Turner first to gauge what the situation was and go from there. His experience with escapees was that they would go back to known relatives, associates, but mostly, ex-wives or girlfriends.

He was about two hours from Sanibel, so he called the Sanibel PD to give them a heads up, that an escaped ex-con might be in their area, and he would be looking for him, so any assistance would be appreciated.

Nate called Jose and left a message telling him where he was headed, and he would give him a call once he got closer.

CHAPTER 19

Me, Tracy, and the ex-cops raced over to the apartment, and tried to get close to it, but the flames were too strong for that. If anyone was in there, they were not going to survive that blast.

I turned to the group. "Let's compare notes and find out who came and went out of there. Since last night, I remember he came in at about ten p.m., and she at about midnight, but I don't remember seeing either one of them leaving, all agreed?"

They all looked at each other, and most nodded in the affirmative. Harry said: "I don't remember anyone leaving, throughout the night or this morning."

Tracy was walking in circles, scratching her head. "Guys let's rack our brains, and try to remember who came and went yesterday, as far a maintenance or delivery. Guys, that is where we will have our bomber."

"Good idea, I think we should write our recollection from yesterday in email or notepad, so we can compare, there's nothing we can do about that inferno."

The fire department had arrived, and they were in the process of hosing down the apartment, and waiting for the smoke to clear, in order to enter, search for bodies, and hopefully the cause of the explosion. So, it would be a little while before we had any information since the bomb squad would go in first.

We compared notes, and we were pretty sure we all remembered the same deliveries to the complex, and narrowed it to one pizza delivery, one Door-Dash, one Uber eats, and one flower shop.

There were people milling around, and I walked amongst the different groups to see if I could pick up anything to work with. I heard one man say he had seen Steve at his front door receiving a basket of flowers that had been delivered. He knew it was from a nearby flower shop, because he had recognized the driver and remembered the same driver delivered a bouquet for his wife on her birthday.

I sent the ex-cops to the local pizza shops since they were more familiar with those. I went to the flower shop, and Tracy was online, checking Door Dash and Uber Eats to see what she could uncover.

There were a few people at the flower shop, and I waited patiently to talk to the manager. I introduced myself, and explained that, while I was not law enforcement, I would be better to deal with than them. I would not close down his shop, or interfere with his business, all I wanted was information on the local orders to the apartment complex, and if there were any strange or unusual requests.

He told me there was one call-in, and cash was paid for the delivery, no receipt requested, and it had to be delivered to a local hotel. I asked if their driver was in and was told he was out back, and he was called over so I could talk to him.

I was surprised to see an elderly man, I guessed to be about late seventies or early eighties, coming towards me. He was frail-looking, and seemed like he couldn't walk very fast.

He stuck his elbow out, instead of a handshake, so I did the same. "Sorry, you can never be sure about germs and infectious diseases at my age, name is Arthur Meyer, how can I help you?"

"Well, Arthur, you can tell me about the delivery to the hotel you made yesterday; it would help with the investigation of the bombing. My name is Jose Castillo, a private investigator, pleasure to meet you."

Arthur pondered for a moment: "I thought something was funny, a cash envelope at the front desk down the road, no personalized note on card, was told to leave it blank, and leave it at the front desk."

"Didn't you think that was kind of odd?' I was as curious as he was.

"Absolutely, that's why I asked where the bathroom was, and when I came out, I ragged the puck at the lobby to see who would come down to pick it up, and sure enough a tough looking hombre picked it up and took it to his room. He had Slavic features, for sure, and I overheard him ask for the flowers, and he had a heavy accent, which sounded from the Baltic States."

54

"Could it have been Russian? And did he have any tattoos you could see?" The hair on the back of my neck was starting to bristle.

"Now that you mention it, he did have a lot of tattoos, and you are right, Russian accent probably."

"Arthur, you have been a valuable font of information, much obliged, may I ask why you are working at your age?"

"A few things: poker and golf, to which I am addicted. It costs money to do both, and Social Security doesn't cover much for me, don't get old, my friend, it's not pretty."

I noticed numbers tattooed on his left arm. "Survived the Holocaust, did you?"

"Unfortunately, I did. It's a heavy burden to remember those who perished, and all I have is faint memories."

"I'm so sorry; so many families were broken up." I remembered my family being displaced by the Cuban Revolution, and the ones that stayed behind hoping to bring Cuba back to what it was, and the fate that awaited them.

Arthur's eyes were welling up. "I wished I would have listened to my instinct back then my girl. I wanted us to leave Poland, but I never thought they would come after us there, too. We were sent to separate concentration camps, never to meet again."

I put my hand on his shoulder. "You hang in there you must have survived for a reason."

"Oy vey, what? I have children and grandkids, ran a company, gave to my congregation, what else? What legacy?"

"Arthur, maybe one of your kids will become President, you never know."

"That schmuck? Ha, from your mouth to God's ears."

"Well, nice meeting you, take my card, if you find any information let me know, I can help you out with those green fees, in case you do."

"You got it, young man."

JORGE GOYANES

I was hoping the Russians were just a coincidence; I did not want to wrangle with the Vory again.

CHAPTER 20

After the smoke literally cleared, and the inquisitive mobs disappeared, Tracy had gone up to the Arson Investigator, and worked her charms to keep her in the loop, which meant I was in the loop, too.

She had changed into a different outfit and was showing a bit more cleavage than before. I mentioned to her. "Nice rack there, Trace."

"Look, buddy, you have weapons, you use them, especially at my age. It's only a matter of time before they head south with gravity."

"Hey, no complaints, just appreciating the talents. I am sure if I bared my chest, I would not get the same results you get."

"Only if the Fire Marshall was a swisher, which I don't think he is, considering how he is not looking at my eyes when he is talking to me, they don't raise past my chest."

"Well, at the risk of being politically incorrect, good job using your assets to gain an advantage. Where are Crate and Barrel, anyway?"

Tracy looked at me funnily. "Who in the hell are they?"

"It's from a detective series I read, *Bosch*, by Michael Connelly. It is a pair of old detectives in the book, those two remind me of them."

"They said they were going for a pie and a brew; I'm guessing they mean pizza and a beer."

"Yep, Northerners, that's what they say. Let us get something to eat, so we can compare notes, I don't want them to know more than we do."

We went to the Colombia Restaurant, in Ybor City, there are two others in the Tampa area, but this is the original established in 1905, and it grew just as fast as the cigar factories in the area back then. I told Tracy that an order of *Paella a la Valenciana* was more than enough for two. It is on a bed of rice, with clams, mussels, shrimp, calamari, chicken, pork, olive oil, green peppers, tomatoes, and cooked in wine. We had a bottle of RG Gran Reserva rioja wine, instead of their homemade *Sangria*, and a Flan for dessert.

After we ate, we sat outside to people's watch, and I pulled out an "Antony and Cleopatra" grenadier. "Do you mind?" I asked Tracy.

She pulled out a pack of "Black and Mild" wood tip wine, much to my surprise. "Don't mind if I do myself."

"Let's get the chitchat out of the way, before we do a deep dive into our situation here, what's new with you?"

"Okay, well, lots of surveillance work, boring as it is, but pays well, divorce attorneys are the only ones that come ahead in divorces. You know, as well as I do, in Florida you can get caught fucking a goat, while doing meth and drinking blood, and it's going to be a fifty-fifty split on the domicile, and the larger breadwinner of the two will have to divvy-up the proceeds earned, during the marriage."

I chuckled. "Yes, I know it's true, how are things at home?"

"Not too good, amigo. My lady friend has been complaining that I am gone too much, I'm thinking of going back to men for a change of pace, they are not as needy, just fuck'em a couple of times a week, a blowjob here and there, and they are happy, as a clam no pun intended. How are things with you and your Okie gal?"

"I can't complain, she puts up with me, I am trying to be a bit more sensitive and compassionate. It's a work in progress, she travels a lot for work, so it's nice when we do get together. I brought up marriage early in our relationship, but she said she wanted to give it some time to see if she could get used to a Cuban, her friends warned her about being involved with one of us, so far so good."

A young couple walked by us, dressed to the nines: she was wearing a miniskirt, five-inch heels, and a tank top, that barely contained her large breasts, and he looked like a gym rat, rippled, and lean.

I said: "They keep making them, don't they?"

Tracy coughed and laughed. "Oh, shit, they sure do. I don't know who I would want more."

"All right, let's get back to the apartment complex, and see if they have come up with any information, and we'll try to figure out what the hell is going on, and who put out a hit on these two."

CHAPTER 21

Nate pulled into the Sanibel Public Library parking lot, and took a few minutes to stretch, after driving for a total of four hours. It was a breezy day, the palm fronds were swaying back and forth, like coordinated hula dancers, which helped keep the temperature to a manageable eighty-five degrees, and only seventy five percent on the humidity.

He was glad every day he lived in Florida, he had been up North on occasion, and had seen fall in all its glory. He liked the same year-round weather Florida had, except for the hurricanes.

He went to the front desk, showed his badge, and asked for Miss Turner. The elderly lady, at the front desk, was wearing a name tag with the name Mildred on it. She was a bit startled, but used the intercom to tell Page she was wanted. "Page, dear, there is an officer here from Miami asking for you."

She hung up the handset with a shaky hand, looked up at Nate, and asked nervously: "Is she in any trouble, officer?"

Nate was known for having a smooth voice, and a calming demeanor. He was usually tasked with informing a family that a relative or a loved one had been a victim of a homicide. He dreaded having to tell a family that a fellow officer had been killed, though.

"Trust me, all good my dear just doing some follow-up on a matter down in Miami she is okay, thank you, where do I go to?"

"Oh, thank the Lord! Down the hall, and first door on the left, God bless."

"Likewise, have a great day, and thank you for volunteering."

Mildred blushed like a schoolgirl. "Oh my, you certainly are a policeman, aren't you? You figured out by my age I'm here to volunteer, you are so smart."

Nate winked at her and headed towards the hallway. He arrived at the office that had Page Turner, "Head Librarian" stenciled on the door. He went to knock when he heard footsteps, which could only be made with heels, coming from the other side of the door, he stopped his attempt at knocking, because the door swung open. He had his badge already out.

"Good morning, come on in. How may I be of assistance? I figured it was only a matter of time before someone from Miami would show up."

Page was in a smart grey pantsuit with matching jacket, black ruffled blouse, and at least six-inch black stiletto heels. She was a redhead with green eyes, a fair complexion, and about five and a half feet tall, who reminded Nate of the actress Julianne Moore.

Nate noticed a small welt on her cheek, which concerned him a bit. "Miss Turner, if you would be so kind to let me know if you have heard from your ex, Johnny Norton, recently?"

She made quick pursing of her lips, that she thought Nate did not notice, but he did. Part of his success doing police work was reading people, and he had gotten very good at it, after twenty years at Metro.

"Please, call me Page, detective, no need to be old school." She settled into her chair, trying to look comfortable, and as normal as possible, but Nate knew better.

"Okay, Page it is, even though I am old school, and would prefer to be formal, no big deal. Has he contacted you, at all?"

"Actually, officer, I did notice the news reports, how could I not? But no, nothing at all from him."

"Page, here is my card, call me if he should contact you, he is dangerous. I will be in the general vicinity for a few days, so I can respond fast, pleasure to meet you."

Page stood up and stuck out her hand. "I know he is dangerous, bad temper, that boy, that's why we did not last. No, sir, the pleasure is all mine, take care, and have a wonderful day."

He stopped at Mildred's desk and handed her his card. "Now, Mildred, this is between you and me, but if a man comes looking for

Miss Turner, whom you haven't seen before, you call me right away, okay?"

Mildred clutched her pearls, and looked around, like she wanted to make sure no one was within earshot of their conversation. "Oh, officer, you know, my friend Janice, who volunteers on Monday's, told me that, a day or so ago, a man came in asking for Page, and he was upset that she was not in at that time. You know, with our budget being cut, all the staff are working part time."

"Did she describe him, at all?" Nate's curiosity was perked up.

"She did not get into details, but she said her impression of him was, that he was a "bad boy"." Mildred giggled and blushed at the mention of "bad boy."

Nate winked at her, which made her blush, again. "You've been most helpful, Mildred. Call me if he should come back calling, you hear?"

"Yes, sir, glad to help out." Mildred was beaming, she felt important for the first time in a long time.

As he was walking to his car, Nate knew something did not feel right with Page. He was planning to watch her for a day or so, just in case, but he could not do it by himself, he needed another body to help out.

CHAPTER 22

The apartment complex parking lot had been cordoned off, and all types of agencies were represented there: ATF, FBI, Hillsborough County Sherriff, and, last but not least, the Florida Department of Law Enforcement Naples office, which was headed by Bill Pulliam, whom Tracy had met thru a previous case. Local television stations had reporters buzzing around, like vultures at a roadkill buffet.

Jose and Tracy walked up to the cordoned area, and were stopped by a local cop. "Sorry folks, only law enforcement are allowed past this point."

Tracy pulled a business card from her jeans. "Would you be a sweetheart, and hand that to Mr. Pulliam over there wearing the FDLE jacket, please?" Butter wouldn't melt in her mouth, but she could turn on you like a Cobra in a second, if needed.

The officer wanted to resist, but she was hard to ignore. "Yes Ma'am, right over."

He walked towards the group that Bill was in, and handed the card to a very short man, who was stocky and bald. His staff called him Bullet Bill behind his back, because of his elongated head, which did not match his short stature.

He looked at the card, turned in our direction, and raised his hand with five fingers, indicating he would be over then.

Tracy looked at Jose. "Can you believe he called me, Ma'am? I could give that boy a ride on the Cougar Express, which he would never forget."

"C'mon, Trace, he looks like he'd just got out of the Police Academy, please don't give him that ride, it will ruin him for life."

She punched Jose in the arm. "Okay, boyo, a ride you wish you could take."

"Not anymore, sister, I am smitten with my Okie, from Muskogee."

"Poor thing, somebody should warn her about you damn Cubanos."

"They did and have but, thank goodness, she ignored them."

"Ah, here comes Bill." He waddled over; it was the best way to describe his walk.

"Miss Lewinski, nice to see you again, what brings you to these parts? And who is this gentleman?"

"Good to see you too, Bill, this is Jose Castillo, from Joe Castle Investigations. Coincidentally, we were hired by different parties to do surveillance on the couple, who resided in the apartment in question."

Bill squinted at Jose. "Jose Castillo, I have heard about you from my brothers, at Metro-Dade. A bit of a thorn in their side if I remember correctly."

Jose stuck his hand out to Bill, which Bill shook grudgingly.

"Guess my reputation precedes me. Just doing my best to make sure justice is served, at whatever it takes."

"Yeah, I heard you have code of honor, or ethics, or some strange scale, which you weigh justice on."

"The end justifies the means, I guess."

"I just met you, but stay on the straight, and narrow around here. I will not be as lenient as my friends at Metro."

Jose saluted Bill, yes, Sir!"

"Oh, yeah, and a bit of a smartass too, they said."

"That's me, making friends, and influencing people."

Bill raised the cordon tape. "You two kids, come on over to the command center, I want my team to get whatever information you have. Right now, between the bomb squad, fire marshal, and the FBI we won't be able to set foot in there for a bit, we can't even see who is in there, until the rubble is cleared. All we know is that someone could not be alive after that blast."

Jose could not resist. "Okay, dad, we will do as we're told."

Bill looked at Tracy. "How do you put up with this, jackass?"

"Not easy, but I have raised four kids, and been married three times, so I am used to dealing with infants and idiots."

"Hey, I am right here."

"I'll be here all week." Tracy said, as she poked Jose in the ribs.

They all laughed and headed towards the command center. It was going to be one long night.

CHAPTER 23

Nate called Jose to see if he was available to help him keep an eye on Miss Turner.

"Oye, amigo, what are you doing for the next day or two? Are you still in Tampa?"

"Still am, podnah, we are on standby here, waiting for the authorities to sift thru the crime scene, so there will be nothing to do for a day or so."

"Why don't you come down to Sanibel? I need to keep an eye on Norton's last girlfriend just in case he shows up. I just have a feeling about it, especially after meeting her."

"You've always told me to trust your gut. Can do, should be there in a couple of hours, so send me the info where you are going to be."

"Texting it to you as we speak, see you."

"Got it, on the way, be there in a bit."

I went to Tracy, to tell her what I had found out about the flower delivery.

"So, let me get this straight, a person with a Russian accent ordered flowers to be delivered to his hotel, paid cash, and had nothing on the greeting card attached?"

"That's about right. The last thing we need is to have another twist in this case, Russians? Why?"

I told Tracy about my history with the Russians in Miami, and that we had a tenuous detente where we tolerated the relationship. But we were leery of each, and one did not trust the other, as far as we could throw each another.

"Geezus, Jose! We are going to need a scorecard to keep up with this case: Casinos, Indians, New York Italians, Unions, retired NYPD cops, and now, Russians."

"Don't forget me, you and a dog named, Boo. I am going to make a call before I head to Sanibel, let's see if I can get some insight as to who is behind this."

"You are showing your age there, Jose, referencing Lobo."

"Hey, you knew the reference, too."

I dialed Pushkin, not expecting any information, but figured I'd give the fishing expedition a try anyway.

He picked up on the first ring. "Mister Castillo, how pleasant to hear from you! How might I be of service?"

"Please, call me Jose, no need to be formal. I was wondering if your associates have any interest in the Tampa area, specifically anything to do with the Indian casino here."

He hesitated a bit, which is what I was hoping for to confirm my suspicions.

"Not that I am aware of, Jose, but I will make some inquiries on your behalf, and get back to you if there is anything pertaining to that."

"Okay, I would appreciate it, thank you."

"My pleasure, I am happy to help, have a good day."

I hung up, and I was pretty pleased.

"Well, Tracy, he did not admit to anything, and he wouldn't anyway. But, by not saying much, his delay spoke volumes."

"So, something is going on with them?" It was more of a statement than a question.

"Fraid so, will give that some thought on my drive to Sanibel, will ring you if I get a brainstorm."

"Sanibel? What is going on there? Anything having to do with our case?"

"Nope, I am just going to help a friend who needs another set of eyes to track down an escaped killer down that way."

I had no idea at the time that helping Nate with that surveillance was not going to go well.

CHAPTER 24

Nate had parked at a convenience store, located across the street from Page's house. He had gone in, and flashed his badge at the owner, and told him that he would be parked there for a while. The owner asked him if there was going to be any trouble.

"Not as long as I can help it." He asked for a large cup of coffee, since he thought it was going to be a long day.

"Would you like anything special in your coffee?" The owner asked.

"Just black, like me. I don't need five hundred calories in a chocolate chip cream mocha frappuccino; I'm just trying to watch my girlish figure."

The owner chuckled, he told him if he needed anything to just ask and that the bathroom was located in the back of the store, and he was free to use it.

"Much obliged, with that coffee I will certainly have the need to go."

Nate settled in his car, as comfortable as he could. He started checking his emails and messages, while keeping a sight line to Page's house.

After a few hours, an Amazon delivery truck pulled up to the curb in front of Page's house. He could not see the driver exiting the truck but figured it would be a quick delivery.

He texted his location to Jose, figuring he should be within thirty minutes by now if he left shortly after they had talked.

He read a few more emails, and sent a text to his assistant Buck, to inquire about the phone search on the last victim. He looked up expecting to see the truck gone, but it was still there. He racked his brain to figure out how much time had passed since the truck arrived, and he was pissed-off at himself for being so careless.

"Shit, shit, shit." He said, as he exited his car, and started sprinting towards the truck. He approached the driver's door of the truck, and slowly slid it open. He looked towards the back, and saw a pair of feet first, and noticed a pool of blood under the body, and what looked like blue dye on the walls of the truck and packages.

He hesitated between going right in, or going back to the store, and asking the owner to call 911. He did the latter, thinking Johnny was not going to harm Page, just probably getting ready to bolt, and maybe getting her credit cards to facilitate his escape. He made his decision in five seconds.

He started running out of gas, on the way back to the store. He thought to himself about getting back into shape, those ten pounds were slowing him up.

While he was running towards the counter, he saw the owner watching a news bulletin on the television. He yelled at the owner to call 911, and to tell them prison escapee, Johnny Norton, was across the street. He bent over, trying to catch his breath, because he was hyperventilating.

The owner said he would, but that the First National Bank of Sanibel had been robbed about thirty minutes ago, and since the SIPD was a small force, it might take them a while to respond.

"Call them anyway, I gotta go!" He took a deep breath and sprinted out the door.

As Nate was approaching the house from the side, he concluded that if Johnny had robbed the bank, he would not need any money, so the only reason he would be back at Page's was for something else, revenge? Getting a hostage? Nate forced himself to mentally slow down his thoughts, and his breathing.

He saw a side window, and grabbed a nearby milk crate and used it to peek in the house. He saw Johnny on top of Page, on the living room floor. His pants were down by his ankles, and he was trying to raise her skirt at the same time. She did not appear to be fighting him, but Nate did not know if she was going along with the inevitable, knowing

Johnny's propensity for violence. There was a gun on the floor next to them, not two feet away.

Nate made his way to the front door, hoping it was not locked. He preferred to not bust it open, alerting Johnny of his presence. Luckily, it was not locked. Nate steeled himself, and charged in, hoping to get the jump on them.

CHAPTER 25

Jose was turning Mother, making a right onto Periwinkle Way after as he entered the island while playing a Joe Sample CD, when his phone rang with a call from Tracy.

He pressed the receive call on the steering wheel, which sent the call thru the radio.

"Hey, what's up? Any new information on the apartment?"

"Jose, take a deep breath, you are not going to believe this, but when the Fire Department finally went into the rubble to look for bodies, they found none, none."

"Are you shitting me? How is that possible? We were watching the whole time."

"Well, except in the middle of the night. I am sure all of us might have dozed off, thinking they were in for the night, I know, I did, dammit! I checked with the retired cops, and while they hemmed and hawed about it, I am sure they dozed off, too."

"Son of a bitch! Tracy don't beat yourself up about it, no way to know that we tried. I'll pull over, and send you my CCTV tape, and check it to see if we missed anything, hold on."

I pulled into Jerry's Grocery store's parking lot and sent her the CCTV footage. I was getting worried about Nate not answering my call or text.

"Tracy, I just sent you the tape, I'll do tracer on Gina's car when I get a chance. I gotta go, later."

"Don't bother, her car is still there."

"Wow, curioser and curioser, okay, I should be here one day tops. In the meanwhile, I will get my IT guy to start scouring Gina's and Steve's credit card purchases for any travel plans, or burner phone purchases. It's a long shot, but it's all I can think of at the moment."

"Is there anything I can do, before you get back?"

"Check to see if there's a back way out of the apartment complex. Hang tight, and we'll put our heads together, and see if we can make neither hide nor hair of this imbroglio."

"A what? Is that one of those fifty-dollar words you use on occasion?"

"Never mind, it means a mess, gotta use that college education for something, will text when I am headed back, keep an eye on those New York cops."

"Hey, I just remembered I have to follow-up on the Uber Eats delivery last night, I will look into that."

"Great idea, keep me posted, gotta go."

Jose brought up the GPS, and saw he was not far away, maybe five minutes, depending on the traffic.

He texted his estimated arrival time to Nate. He called Gafford, and he was surprised that he answered at all. He usually lets calls go to voice mail first, to see if it is something he wants to deal with.

"Hey, you answered right away, thanks."

"I saw it was you, Keemosabe. I know you are on a case, and I did offer to help you as always, you know I live vicariously thru you."

"Ha, I live thru you, amigo. No worries, no mortgage, no rug rats, bohemian lifestyle, no ball and chain, you are living the dream."

"Well, I will have to bring you up to date over a cold one. I stuck my ankle out and think it's going to have a chain on it soon. We'll have to do dinner with her when Kat gets back."

"Mazel Tov, what's her name?"

"Rosalita, met her at a software seminar last month, we appear to be hitting it off, after two dates."

"Great, will do, she sounds Hispanic."

"Yep, Cuban, fiery personality, loves to dance."

"Uh oh, they have a temper, and are the jealous type, be careful. Dancing? I'll pay money to see you dance."

"Okay, enough, you are messing with me. What can I help you with?"

"I will email you the particulars on the two people I am tailing here. I think they created their own kidnapping or disappearance, so try to track travel plans, last phone calls, or burner phone purchases."

"I'm on it, will do, catch you soon, and thanks for the congratulations."

"Hey, no problema Amigo, I will be looking into a Tux for the wedding."

"No tux, Hawaiian shirts only. Now, kindly fuck off, J.C., goodbye."

I thought about Tracy's call and tried to make some sense of it. There were no bodies in the rubble, so they did not plan their own demise. It would require having two corpses, and with today's technology, it would not take long to see thru that subterfuge. Did they know someone was after them, and got out in the nick of time?

I arrived at the location, according to the GPS, and pulled up behind an Amazon truck, which had been parked in front of the house. I called Nate, but there was no answer, my sense immediately picked up that something was wrong.

I retrieved a Glock from the gun safe and headed towards the house.

CHAPTER 26

Nate charged thru the door with gun drawn, and to say the couple on the floor was surprised was an understatement. Johnny was still on top of the woman, and tried twisting to his right, trying to get off of her. His pants were by his ankles, and he was trying to pull them up.

"Don't move or I will blow your head off!" Nate yelled at the top of his voice, concentrating on Johnny, while taking small steps towards the couple, remembering that Johnny said he would not be taken alive.

"Thank God, officer! I thought I was going to die!" Yelled Page at a higher voice than Nate thought she should have used.

The gun on the floor was on the right side of Page, and Nate made a few steps towards it hoping to kick it away, all the while keeping an eye on Johnny.

Page said: "I'll take care of that gun detective, just keep yours on him."

By now, Nate was six feet away from them, and kept his gun pointed at Johnny ready to fire if he made a sudden move.

Johnny tried to get up on his elbows, but Nate told him: "One more move, and I will help you keep your promise of not being taken alive."

It was the last thing he said, as Page picked up the gun, and fired directly at Nate's chest.

Nate was stunned, started falling backwards as he felt he was hit in the chest by a sledgehammer, before blacking out.

Jose was just rushing thru the door when he saw this unfold before him.

He saw the girl shoot Nate, and Johnny was already up on his knees, trying to get up.

Jose shot the girl in the head and then aimed his gun at Johnny. "You're next, Motherfucker! Make your move!"

Johnny looked at Page and was incredulous. "You, son of a bitch you killed her!" He yelled.

"What did you expect, asshole? She shot, not only a cop, but my friend!"

"Fuck you! Fuck you! And fuck you!" Johnny yelled.

"So, you must be Norton a career criminal, mean streak, abuser of animals, and murderer. You said they won't take you alive, well, what's it going to be?"

"You can't kill me, I have no weapon, I am not charging you, and how will that look?"

"Think I care about a lowlife like you? You should have been put down, like the animals, and people you have done the same to. I thought you didn't want to be taken alive?"

"Well...I...I..." Johnny stammered.

"Ah, so now you're not such a tough guy, are you? Telling everyone in the joint that you would not be taken alive, typical bully, blowhard, shooting off your mouth halfcocked, trying to come off as a swinging dick."

"Fuck you, asshole! Show me your badge, you don't look like a cop to me."

"My badge is right here, locked and loaded in my hand."

"Show me your badge! I won't ask you again."

"Johnny, boy, you are not in a position to request anything." Jose could hear the sirens getting closer, so he decided to act fast, when he heard Nate moaning.

"Say hello to the other side, asshole. You don't deserve to walk this planet, like the rest of us."

"You can't! It's not fair, not fair, I have rights!" Johnny was sweating and shaking.

"Like the people you've killed, Johnny boy?" Jose said, as he fired right into Johnny's chest.

Johnny had a momentary look of confusion, as he dropped like a sack of rice.

"What just happened?' Nate said weakly, from his position on the floor.

"Just taking out the trash Amigo." Jose saw Johnny had a knife strapped to his ankle; he laid it by Johnny, making sure he handled it so his prints wouldn't be on it.

Nate opened his shirt, and took the slug, which was embedded in his vest. He was glad he wore it, even though it was uncomfortable and brutally hot in the heat and humidity.

"Geezus Christ! I am going to be sore for a while." He took off his vest and saw a bruise on his chest.

They could both hear the sirens coming and knew the law would be arriving soon.

"We will talk about this, after everything is settled. I did not like what I thought I saw, let's go outside, and put our guns on the ground. The cops in this area are known for having happy trigger fingers."

"Especially, since we are both minorities, me being Cuban and all."

Nate chuckled. "Yeah, who do you think they'll shoot first, Tonto? You, who could pass the "whitey" smell test from a mile away? Or, a charcoal skinned, nappy haired bastard like me?"

They went outside and sat on the stoop with the guns on the ground a couple of feet away from them, Nate was holding his badge up in the air, and Jose doing the same with his P.I. badge.

CHAPTER 27

Sheriff Brady Judds, of Lee County, was a no-nonsense lawman, who had been elected on a law and order platform. He had cleaned up meth labs, street dealers, and incoming drug shipments from offshore ships then offloaded onto smaller boats. They would try to sneak in thru the mangrove filled jetties between Sanibel/Captiva and the mainland.

His methods were heavy-handed, but crime had steadily dropped since he had taken office. Every drug bust had come with a corresponding press conference with his heavily armed and masked SWAT team, placed behind him for the cameras to see with the drugs, guns, and cash that they recovered.

Judds, Nate, and Jose were sitting at the dining room table, while there was a beehive of activity in the living room between the crime photographers, forensics team, and evidence technicians. Nate looked at his watch, and saw it was coming around to eight o'clock.

Judds with a skeptical look on his face, said directly to Nate: "So, just to go over this one more time for clarity: you staked out Miss Turner's home, and notified the Sanibel P.D., which is proper protocol, got lucky Norton was using her, and you caught them in the act, she shot you much to your surprise, and you had the wherewithal to call your buddy to help you with the surveillance. So, he arrived just in the nick of time, like the cavalry, to save your ass and kill Norton, and the girl must have given the gun to Norton somehow before she was shot, correct?"

"You almost everything right, just want to reiterate that Jose saw Norton grabbing the gun from the girl and he fired because he was afraid for his life."

Judds chuckled. "Yeah, Castillo, looks like he could twist Norton into a pretzel, if he desired so."

Jose put his hand up. "Under the circumstances, and with the charged atmosphere, seeing Nate on the floor, and knowing Norton's history of violence, I was afraid for my life, and shot at him in self-defense."

"Yeah, sure, well said. You know the Florida stand your ground law well, just like a defense attorney." Judds spit some tobacco into a cup he was holding.

"You know that stuff will kill you, if you don't watch out." Jose tried to be funny.

"Thanks, but I don't think I will take advice from someone who appears to be a vigilante and has a history of it. In fact, your buddy Nate here arrested you once, for a similar situation." Judds pointed to Nate.

"Ah, I see you've looked me up. So, you know the charges didn't stick after the State Attorney dropped them, and I received a commendation and key to the city from the mayor." Jose had crossed his arms on his chest, and quickly unfolded them, knowing his body language would show that Judds was getting under his skin.

"Remind me to request an eight by ten glossy of you, so I can take it to the shooting range for target practice." Judds stood up. He did have a bit of a sense of humor. "Okay, gentlemen, unless forensics shows anything different from what you've told me, you are free to go. We know where you can be reached. And, by the way, Castillo, be careful smoking those Cuban cigars we saw in your van, you know that stuff will kill you."

Jose got up, he extended his hand to Judds. "A wise guy, huh?"

"It takes one to know one." He shook Jose's hand and turned to Nate. "I hope you haven't put your career online for this jackass. Take care of yourself and hopefully I won't have to be in touch."

Nate shook the sheriff's hand. "Appreciate the professional courtesy, if you are ever down my way, consider a favor owed. "

Judds chuckled. "I would rather have root canal without Novocain, than to have to go down to the modern Sodom and Gomorrah."

"C'mon, sheriff, it's not that bad, we were both raised down there, and we did not turn out too bad." Jose said, as he patted Judds on the back.

"I'll wait to pass judgment on that, Castillo. You two show up, and we have the first shootings here in years, get out of here, before something else happens."

Jose saluted. "Yes, sir, right away."

Judds looked at Nate. "How do you put up with this asshole?"

"Trust me, it's an acquired taste." Nate winked at Jose.

Jose and Nate went to Mother to cool off. Jose poured two drinks, made from Captain Morgan, and a splash of diet tonic water, with a wedge of lime.

"Diet tonic? Really?" Nate said.

"Just trying to watch my weight, you should too. You are getting pudgy there, amigo."

"Fuck you, drink up, we have to talk."

"Fire away, my friend, what do you have?"

"Even though, I was groggy and just coming around, it appeared to me that you shot Norton without provocation."

"Like I said, I was afraid for my life. You don't know what happened, before you came around, he would have killed me, given the chance."

"But did he ever have the chance? Only thing you are afraid of is your ex-wife, you are bullshitting me."

"Oh damn! Don't bring her up, will ya? Listen, he would have gotten back into the system, put away for life, and try to escape again, one worthless human being voted off the island."

"Jose, why do you put yourself as final arbiter of someone's life? Doesn't it wear on you?"

"Guess not, my friend. You know he was not the first, and probably won't be the last. By the way, you're welcome for saving your life, I can live with my actions, I have so far."

"So far, you say, if you ever need to talk, you know I am always here for you. And by the way, thanks for saving my life, now we are even since I saved yours once."

"Pay for dinner at Ruth Chris' steakhouse, you cheap bastard, that's a start."

"Slainte, deal, you gotta go back to Tampa, get out of here." They both chuckled, and clinked glasses.

Nate headed towards his car, and was deciding whether to make the drive home, and start doing the paperwork on the case, or instead check in to a motel and rest. He decided on the latter and headed towards I-75 to check in to one of the many hotels located off the exits.

Jose hung up the hammock he kept in Mother, set his alarm for one hour, and took a catnap, before heading back to Tampa. He wished he had time to stop off, to see his friends at The Dunes Golf and Tennis Club while in Sanibel, but knew he had to get back to Tampa.

CHAPTER 28

David had decided to wait for Monica inside her apartment. Since he had already made a copy of her key, it was just a matter of waiting for her to come home. The apartment had two bedrooms, one which was used as an office, so he planned to wait for her in that room's closet.

At seven o'clock, he heard the jangle of keys, and instantly perked up. He heard the clickety-clack of her heels on the tile floor and wondered which shoes she had on. Before going into hiding in the spare room, he had gone to her closet, and fondled and smelled some of her shoes. He went into her laundry basket and did the same with her underwear.

He had to control himself, from wrapping some of her panties around his fully erect penis, and jack-off. But he was saving the first shot of cum for her.

Listening to her movements got a little tough since she had taken her heels off but was okay once he heard the shower being turned on, he knew where she was.

He waited a few minutes, before coming out of the closet. He had already changed into his full body wetsuit. He had taken to a seamstress and asked her to put a zipper in the crotch. When she told him that it would not be waterproof and suggested that it would leak, he told her he had prostate issues, and when he had to pee, he could not wait to take the suit off, and needed he fast access.

With the suit on, and the hoodie covering his head, the chances of him leaving any hairs were minimal since he was fully shaved. He liked the feeling of different cloth textures in that area, but also less hair meant the chances of leaving evidence was cut by a lot. He had watched enough crime shows to know a strand of hair, found at a crime scene, could derail the perfect crime, but he felt he had prepared for that.

He stood to the left of the bathroom door, and had a cloth soaked with ether in his right hand. He heard the curtain rustle and took a breath to calm himself down. He put on his surgical mask, when heard her steps, and geared to smother her and knock her out as soon as she stepped out the bathroom door.

Monica stepped out of the bathroom and caught something out of the corner of her eye, but she was taken down, and smothered so fast she couldn't get a scream out.

David had the move down to perfection, cloth on the mouth and nose, trip her with his leg and his left hand was on the back of her head. He wound up on top of her as he was pushing her down. His cloth was so saturated, that it did not take long to render her unconscious.

CHAPTER 29

Jose called Gafford, as soon as he guided Mother towards Tampa. He asked how the phone scan was going, and if he had any hits yet.

Gafford explained that it was a long search, since there were thousands of calls from the known victims and cross referencing the calls required, creating a program to do so. It had been created by one of his hacker cronies as a favor, and it was actually running as of the previous day.

He told Jose that he expected a report within twenty-four hours, and he would send him an email, as soon as it was finished.

Thinking it would ease Nate's mind, he left him a voice mail indicating that there might be a lead coming up soon.

He called Tracy to tell her he was on the way back, and to get an update on things.

"Well, bucko, not much going on here; no sight of the couple, no airplane tickets, hotels used, their phones are either dead or turned off, and no credit cards used. It's like they vanished into thin air."

"That is so strange, I can't put my finger on what this is all about."

"Any leads on the deliveries around the apartment?"

"A few things, dough and nuts have been most helpful, they've found a few bits of info."

"Dough and nuts, who is that Trace?"

"Oh, the guys you called Crate and Barrel, figured they needed their own monikers. So, after watching them eat donut after donut, I gave them the names Dough and Nuts, get it? Doughnuts?"

"You have a sick sense of humor, sister, what did they come up with?"

"Well, you know about the flowers, the pizza delivery was from a shop all the way across town, which is odd considering there are at least three pizza shops a stone's throw away from here. The pizza was delivered to the apartment next door to Gina's. But I interviewed the neighbors and they said they didn't order it, but the driver told them it was pre-paid, so they took it.

"Wow, Trace, this is getting weirder and weirder."

"Tell me about it, but wait, there's more."

"Geezus, I'm afraid to ask."

"The neighbors remembered hearing door knocks at Gina's, it went on for a few minutes, but they don't remember a conversation, or the door opening. The man peeked, and remembered he saw flowers and a food order by Gina's front door. And here's the kicker, Door Dash had an order for Gina, which was paid with a gift card. Hard to trace, I am trying to contact the restaurant to see how it was placed, they don't have cameras, but the girl that took the order is working the night shift tonight, so I will go talk to her."

"So, let me see if I got this right, since there are a lot of moving parts. Flowers were paid for in advance, and delivered to a hotel, where a European-looking man picked them up. A pizza was ordered from a shop across town, pre-paid, and the delivery instructions were to the apartment next door to Gina's. Door Dash had an order also to Gina's apartment, and at this time we do not know who ordered it, but we should have some information on all that soon."

"That's about right, J.C."

"Good job, you and the doughnuts, try to get a timeline. There's got to be some tie-in to all of this, a mystery wrapped around an enigma."

"Well put, Jose, you should consider writing at some point."

"Very funny, they tell you to write what you know about, so a mechanic that moonlights as a P.I. will never fly."

"Jose, think about it, what are you doing right now? You are working as a P.I. and restoring cars for a living."

"Not going to happen, Trace, no time, no talent."

"You'd be surprised. You can finally use those fifty-dollar words you are always throwing around."

"Yes, I would finally get to use some of the college experience at the U, before I was kicked out of there."

"You went to the University of Miami? Really?"

"Yes, indeed, two semesters on a tennis scholarship, before I got kicked out."

"Oh, do tell, crazy parties having anything to do with getting thrown out?"

"Pretty close there, another time for that story, what else you got?"

"A man came looking for you, his name was Arthur, and he said he had some information for you, but would not tell me what it was."

"That's great, Tracy, he works for the flower shop delivering. I will check with him when I get back, thanks, see you in a few."

CHAPTER 30

I hung up with Tracy, then I called Gafford.

"Hey, Bud, I know you have a lot on your plate, but check the casino's corporation, and see if there is any stock movement, like insider trading or a hostile takeover going on, anything that does not look above board."

"Will do, but the phone log came back sooner than we thought. I am sending it to you by email, I took a glance at it, and three of the victims had four phone numbers in common they all called regularly within a two-year span. You will have to sort out what the coincidence is, and if there is a tie-in, they were a nail-shop, a beauty parlor, a gym, and an auto dealership."

"Great Jim, this will help a lot, do you have any problems with me sending it to Nate? It will save him a lot of time."

"No problem, but remember I got the list without a warrant, so it cannot be used as evidence and, of course, it's illegal as hell."

"I am sure Nate will know where I got the list from, and he knows from whom, and he will be discreet."

I called Nate, and he answered with: "Ruth Chris' steakhouse, how may I help you?"

"You are going to pay for a meal there, you cheap bastard, especially after what I am going to give you."

"Oh, then how about Lotto numbers? Stock tips? Football picks? Jennifer Aniston's phone number?"

"I will email you a phone call log of the last three victims of your serial killer, the phone numbers they all had in common within the last two years. You will have to sort them out and see if it ties into someone who they all knew or dealt with."

"Great, you must have had Gafford on it, my people are still trying to get authorization from the phone companies for the logs. Knowing

Gafford, I am sure it was not done legally, but I'll get around that somehow. Dinner will be on me if this pans out."

"Good, appreciate that. Just remember that he can't testify or divulge how he got the list."

"No problema, amigo. I'll keep our authorization request open, and make it look like we got it from the phone company."

"Well, look there, my best friend is bending the rules a little bit, I'm proud of you Nate, there's still hope for you."

"Never, and nowhere as bad as you, Jose."

"Always a first time, hope you can live with yourself."

"Hey, it's for the greater good, catching a bad guy always is."

"Now, you know how I feel about it, you've made my case for me."

"Yeah, but there's a line I will not cross, I will not shoot anyone without provocation, I took an oath,"

"Good for you. Unfortunately, we won't be sharing box seats in Heaven, I took an oath too, but resigned, as you well know. It was comforting to know I could take out bad guys without that oath, and shield holding me back."

"Heaven? Shit, you believe in Heaven and Hell?"

"Hell is right here; you know that from your job. Heaven, really? That is the good times we make here, nothing after that but a void, like a Black Hole in the universe."

"Well, well, Jose, looks like we have some nice discussions coming up at dinner, then."

"Yeah, Ruth Chris' don't forget."

"Fuck off, will probably be at McDonald's."

"See you, you cheap bastard."

CHAPTER 31

Monica was slowly coming around dazed and confused, as to what was happening to her. She was hoping it was a bad dream, but her body told her otherwise.

She had a gag ball in her mouth. Her hands were tied to the bed with ropes, and the ropes ended at handcuffs on each wrist. The handcuffs had velvet wraps, she guessed that was to keep her wrists from bruising. She was sore between her legs, and her anus did not feel the same.

The smell of Clorox, or some like chemical, permeated her body, like she'd been saturated in it.

She knew that she was helpless, and hoped this was the worst of it. She was starting a prayer, when she saw a figure coming into the bedroom, holding a cup of coffee in one hand, and a syringe in the other. He was wearing a wetsuit, galoshes, surgical gloves, and had a full-face medical mask on.

She was an unwilling part of a horror movie and started shaking.

He came, sat beside her on the bed, and stroked her hair gently.

"Shh...shhh be still my lovely." His voice was familiar, but in her condition, she was not able to place it.

He cleared his throat. "You have been a very good girl, you didn't fight much, and in fact, based on your orgasms, you seemed to enjoy it, which pleases me much. You know the thing about the human body, is that it will welcome stimulation, no matter the conditions. I must say you are the best of all of them...so far."

He held up the syringe "I noticed you have some Valium, and I've made a little concoction here to help you sleep it off."

"Oh, my God!" she thought, this lunatic has done this before. She wondered how many he had done this to.

"Now, now, my dear. I am going to take the ball out for one moment for you to tell me one thing you want before you go to sleep.

Something reasonable within the confines of this game, one thing, and of course it can't be your freedom, maybe a pillow, a stuffed animal over there, a picture of your parents."

She felt she was going to faint, and she thought she'd recognized his voice, she was not sure, but that snapped her back to reality.

"Nod your head, when you are ready to tell me about that one wish."

Monica nodded her head; she knew what she wanted. She was not sure about the voice, but what the hell she thought, if it wasn't him, he could prove his innocence if indeed he was.

He gently pulled the ball from her mouth. "What is it, my dear? What will it be?"

She whispered: "my car keys."

He laughed, and placed the ball back in her mouth "Oh dear, okay, you think you'll need those? You got it, coming right up."

He retrieved the keys from her purse and gave them to her.

Monica made sure out of all the keys on her chain, she had a firm grip on her car keys, hoping they would draw some blood, maybe some smart detective would see it as a clue, a futile attempt at this point, since she knew she was going to die anyway, but at least it was something.

"It has been more than a pleasure my darling, sleep well."

He put the rag with ether over her nose, waited until her eyes closed and her breathing labored before he placed the syringe into the vein in her arm. He checked for a pulse after a few minutes, and finding none, he took the ball out of her mouth, and started to prep for his exit.

He took off his wet suit, changed into street clothes, put on the grey colored wig, got her vacuum cleaner out, and proceeded to vacuum the bedroom and bathroom. He took the vacuum cleaner bag out and put it in his bag. He had brought a portable Vac, which he used to clean the hoses and base of her vacuum cleaner. He went to the tub and used his Vac at the drain as a precaution, even though he had let the shower run for thirty minutes, after he had cleansed her.

He washed the coffee cup and placed it in the sink. He looked back at Monica and sighed. "It's been wonderful my lovely."

After he closed the front door, he took off his gloves, and headed into the night.

CHAPTER 32

I started checking my messages and voice mails, on the way to Tampa. There were the usual sales pitches, and car warranty extension updates, that I deleted.

There were several messages and texts from my contact John Bond at the casino, wanting updates. The messages got a more intense from the first to the last one received, which had been a few hours ago, while the wrap-up had ended in Sanibel.

I returned his call first and brought him up to date on what we did and didn't know, and told him I was headed back to Tampa, and that I would gather any new information and pass it on to him. I also asked him how long it would take him to get his Board together, in case I wanted to meet with them, and discuss the case.

He was a bit perplexed at my request and asked why. I said that once I had all the information, I would prefer to give my report in person, that way there would be no way to misinterpret things, and to give a chance to answer any questions.

He reluctantly agreed, saying he would need a few hours notice to get the Board together. I told him I would give him a day's notice, and that I might be bringing some folks with me who could help clear up the situation. I had a plan starting to percolate, and I was going to bring an odd group together.

No sooner than I hung up with Bond, I received a call from Gafford.

"Give me some good news, buddy."

"Bad news first, Keemosabe. No digital trace from the couple after the bombing, just like they fell off the Earth, not even Sunpass activity going thru any tolls."

"Means they must have taken back roads out of town, what's the good news?"

"Good news is, there's a handful of calls' prior to them disappearing, and of course being the inquisitive guy that I am. I did some phone tracing. The calls to and from Gina's phone were to a restaurant in Brooklyn, and a spa in Miami Beach."

"Curiouser and curiouser again, have any names attached to those phones? And were the calls outgoing or incoming?

"Very easy to figure out. The restaurant in Brooklyn is owned by an LLC that, after all is peeled away, it's owned by Gina's father, that one was outgoing. The spa, as you probably figured out, is owned by our Russian friends, and that one was incoming,"

"Geezus Mary, and Joseph, what a tangled web we weave! I'm going to need a scorecard to sort this mess out. I have an idea, her car is still at the apartment, so check with DMV, and see if there's a car registered in his name, and if there is, can you track it?"

"Good idea, J.C.! I actually thought of doing that, get back to you in a few. If he has a newer car with a smart key, I can literally hijack it with my system."

"Please do that, catch you later. Let me know what store the Bridal registry will be, okay?"

"Fuck off, J.C., later."

CHAPTER 33

Arriving at the apartment complex, I located Tracy, and we went looking for the Doughnuts. Ironically, they were chowing down at the diner that had become our unofficial office.

Tracy and I sat with them, ordered, and then I brought everyone up to speed.

Vinnie and Harry were on the cholesterol train to hell, after looking at their plates: Eggs, sausage, biscuits, bacon, bagels, ham steaks, and cherry Danishes.

"Boys, I hope your Wills are current, you keep eating like that, and it won't be long before you're pushing up daisies." I had to say something, it was crazy.

Vinnie piked in first. "Jose, we talked about it. We're both divorced, our kids are grown, and we have no grandchildren. So, we decided to go out in style, eating and drinking to our hearts content, so fuck off!"

"Geez, man, that's the third time, in the last few hours, I have been told to fuck off. There must be something in the air."

"Imagine that, what a shock, must be your making friends and influencing people demeanor." Tracy was smiling, like a Cheshire cat.

Harry almost choked on his biscuit. "Girl, you give it out good, will try to keep from riling you up."

The waitress brought a salad for Tracy and a turkey BLT for me.

Vinnie elbowed Harry. "Look there, healthy eating, what a concept."

I decided to keep us on course. "There is a lot more to this than meets the eye. I do not think everything is as it has been shown to us, we have a call from the Russians to the couple, which opens a whole can of worms, a call from Gina's phone to her father, asking for help maybe. There were no calls to or from the Casino, which is odd. It has to all be related, don't know how at the moment, any thoughts?"

Harry sat back in his chair, put his hands on his ample stomach, and belched, like a tugboat's horn. "Excuse me, but it is hard to tell who the good guys are from the bad guys, and what is everyone after, and who the hell are the Russians?"

"The Russians are from Miami Beach, whom I've had some dances with over time. They are into everything down there and are looking to expand their reach. I know that the casino hired me to look after the couple, because Steve is on their board being one of the Osceola's. I'm wondering if the Russians are trying to get their claws slowly into the casino, and Esposito has a financial interest in his company's supplying food, liquor, and laundry services, and don't forget the Union probably has an interest, too."

My phone rang, and it was Gafford calling.

"Good call, Boss. I picked up his car, a Jeep Cherokee, from the GPS on board, and it has just left the Immokalee casino heading South on U.S. 27. The GPS on the Jeep has the Tribe reservation address on it, so I'm assuming that is where they are headed to. I'll send you the vehicle info, so you know what to look for."

"Well done, thanks. Probably headed to Big Cypress reservation, keep up the good work, later."

"One more thing, the casinos are owned solely by the tribe, so they control the Board, and a side company called "Indian Gaming," it's a closed culture, hope that helps."

"So, there's no way to buy stock, or do a hostile takeover, huh?"

"Nope, only way to do it would be to make an offer, so over the value that it would be hard to turn down. So, guess not much help, then?"

"Actually, it takes one of my theories out, so more to figure out. Thanks again, Jim, later."

I turned to the group. "Okay, kids, here's the plan: Tracy, you follow up with the girl who took the food order from Door Dash and see what you can find out. You two, go to the pizza shop, and see if you can find out anything at all that would help. I am going to the Big Cypress reservation, where I am sure the couple is heading, we'll keep in touch, and plan on meeting back here tonight."

Harry put in his two cents worth. "Great idea to meet back here, they have liver and onions on special tonight."

Vinnie turned to him. "You just ate and thinking of dinner, already? I thought I was bad."

Tracy made a funny face. "Eww, liver and onions? That's disgusting, it's an animal's organ!"

I couldn't help it. "Tracy, I am sure that is not the first organ you didn't like eating."

Vinnie and Harry couldn't stop laughing.

"Castillo, you are a pig, go to hell!"

"Been there, done that, got the tee shirt."

"Let's go, gang, be careful out there, and see you tonight."

I fired up Mother, and headed south, trying to figure out this tangled web. I called John Bond at the Casino, since he did hire me to bring him up to speed, and I told him that the meeting would not be at his offices, but rather at the Big Cypress reservation. He told me he could be there, in less than an hour. I told him it would be a good idea for him to be there. The more the merrier, I thought.

CHAPTER 34

I arrived at the reservation, and asked to see Billy Powell, or Sam Jones. I was directed to the Tribal Council office, but was told there had been an incident, and the Tribal police was in charge, and to check in with Captain Fernandez, when I arrived there.

I pulled up to the main building, where there was a cruiser with the blue lights flashing. I got out of the car, and I saw the vehicle belonging to Steve, with a male body lying on the ground next to it. Billy Powell was hugging Gina, who was sobbing uncontrollably into his arms.

A uniformed officer was talking to Sam Jones, who was a few feet away. The blood by the body was still pooling, so it was fairly fresh.

I walked close to the body and saw there was a gun being held in the right hand of the corpse, it was Steve Osceola. I walked around the vehicle to see if anything was awry and saw a set of golf clubs in the back seat, and two suitcases in the back.

"Hey you! Get away from there! There's evidence we don't want disturbed." It was the uniformed officer who was talking to Sam Jones, and she was walking towards me with an attitude.

"Who the hell are you? Show me some I.D., please. I'm Captain Arley Fernandez, and I am in charge here."

I was taken aback by the captain. She was definitely of Hispanic origin, probably Cuban or Rican, she was small in stature, and had a build like someone who pumped iron.

She took my P.I. license and looked me up and down. "I've heard you; you are that pain in the ass P.I. from Miami. I remember your name being mentioned when I was a rookie at Miami Beach P.D., something to do with the Vory, unpleasant situation if I remember, and the gang at Metro either hated you, or used you when convenient."

"Ah, it's tough being semi-famous. My reputation does precede me, helping damsels in distress, or helping cops find their ass using two hands."

"Yes, you were a cop once, weren't you? Still full of yourself, I see, the asshole description is warranted."

"A long time ago in a galaxy far, far away, Captain."

"Couldn't take the heat, so you got out of the kitchen?"

"No, I couldn't take the bureaucracy, red tape, politics, and soft judges. Justice is blind, but they've also tied her hands behind her back."

"Strangely, I agree, that's why I left Beach P.D. Here, we are self-governing, and self-policing, even the Feds find it hard to fuck with us. So, what brings you here?"

"I am working on this case, ask Sam and Billy over there." I nodded to the two, who were now both holding Gina up.

"Let's go over there, and sort this out. As you can see, her boyfriend is dead, and Gina shot him in self-defense according to her."

As we were walking back, I dropped my car keys next to the body. I knelt down and looked at his left hand. Just I as suspected, there were calluses on it.

"Hey! Get away from that body! I haven't even gotten around to it yet. One more time, and I'm going to cuff you, Christ on crutches!" Arley was hopping mad.

"Sorry, Cap'n just dropped my keys."

"Sorry my ass, Castillo, knock it off!"

"At the risk of being politically incorrect, a cute ass, if I say so."

"Oh, my fucking God! Ever heard of the "Me Too" movement, asswipe?"

"Nah, the only "me too" movement I hear about is the women who pleases their man, and then have to tell them "me too" you selfish bastard. No wonder, it's a crapshoot out there."

"Good Lord, Castillo. You have just sent the men's movement back to the Mesozoic ages."

I liked her demeanor already, tough as nails with attitude to match, knows her Paleozoic from her Mesozoic eras.

CHAPTER 35

We went into the office, and Sam guided us into a conference room, where he offered coffee or water to the group.

Gina was still sobbing, and Billy asked if we could take a few minutes to let her compose herself, which we agreed to.

I pulled Fernandez to the side and asked her if she could procure Gina's and Steve's phones, in order to see what calls they might have received recently.

Arley stood up, and asked Gina for her phone.

"What the hell for?" Gina asked, wiping her nose between sobs, while handing her phone over.

"Number one, because I asked for it. And, number two, this is a shooting investigation, which I have to determine if it is an accident, a self-defense scenario, or a homicide."

Billy slammed his hand on the table. "A homicide? Are you serious, Captain?"

"I will do the job I am hired to do, Mister Powell. The facts will determine where I go with this, and no one is above the law, even here, you of all people should know that."

Arley headed towards the door. "I'll be right back; I have to check on something."

Sam turned towards me and did not look very happy. "Jose, I am sure once everything is explained, it will pan out. After all, Steve did pull a gun on Gina, she was only defending herself."

I tried not to sound sarcastic. "I have full confidence in the captain, she seems like a no-nonsense person, and she won't be deterred by politics or agendas. You guys did hire her, did you not?"

"Well, of course, she was highly decorated, and recommended by all we interviewed."

Arley stuck her head in the room. "Hey, Castillo. I need your help for a minute, follow me."

Billy got up when I did. "Need any help, Captain?"

"No, just him, and get her under control. When I get back, I will be asking her what happened."

I followed Arley to her cruiser. "Get in and pay attention." Man-o-man, she was bossy.

She had three phones with her. "Here is Gina's, this must be Steve's, and I found this burner phone in the center console, what can you do with them?

"We'll see the last incoming or outgoing calls on all of these. I have a contact who can tell me who those calls were to or from."

"Can they do it quickly? Who the hell do you know at the NSA?"

"Hell Captain, this guy makes the NSA look like amateurs. Write the numbers down, and give me fifteen minutes or so, and we shall see."

"Just call me Arley, until we get back in there. I'm not big on formalities, unless something official is going on."

"Like a shooting that smells funny?"

Arley turned in her seat quickly. "Smells to you too, huh?"

"Yep, these two were so in love or lust, that they concealed their relationship to the casino. They were shacked up together, so something serious must have taken place for her to shoot him."

"Agreed, you know more about them than I do. All I know about Steve, is that he was on the Board of the casino, and he was rumored to lead the tribe as their next leader, why would anyone want him out?"

"Well, that for sure throws a lot of shade on this situation."

CHAPTER 36

I called Gafford and was hoping he was available. "Sorry to bother you, Jim. But unfortunately, I got a bit of a situation I need help with right away."

"Got a few minutes, before I go pick up Rosalita for dinner, what's up?"

I explained the situation and sent him the last numbers that were on all three phones.

"That's all? Man, I can do that with my eyes closed in a few minutes, call you right back."

I called Tracy and gave her the news. I told her to inform the doughnuts that our surveillance was over, to call her contact who hired her, and to expect a ton of questions, which she could not answer at this time.

"No shit, Jose, she shot him?"

"There's no doubt about it, I will be interviewing her with local law enforcement shortly. I will call you as soon as we sort this out, and please don't leave the area, I will be back as soon as some calls are made."

"Alright, Jose, I will hang tight, later."

Good timing, Jim called as soon as I hung-up with Tracy.

"Okay, partner, easy pickings. The phone registered to Gina received a call from a spa in Miami Beach, which is owned by an LLC, registered to a company in Saint Lucia. Gina called a number in Brooklyn, right after that. Steve's phone received a call from a private investigator, based in Tampa, will send you his info shortly. The burner phone being what it is; I can't tell you who they called, but I can tell you it was minutes after Gina made the second call on her phone, got it?"

"Holy smokes, Jim, thanks. I'm going to write notes to keep up with this, stellar work as always. Save me the bill for your dinner with Rosalita, you deserve it."

"Hey, my man, she invited me to dinner at Monty Trainer's in the Grove, it's on her."

"Congrats man, you got a keeper there studly. I'll be your best man, will get my tux ready."

"I'm planning on keeping her for sure. It's you, no doubt; no tux, just sandals, shorts, and Hawaiian shirts."

"Geezus, Jim! Who is performing at the wedding, Pitbull ?"

"Maybe, I'll ask him next time I talk to him."

"Shit, I was just kidding, didn't know you knew him."

"Who do you think sets up the electronics for his concerts?"

"Damn, son! Known you all these years, and you never mentioned him."

"You'd be surprised who I know, I just keep a low profile."

"Well, thanks again, talk soon."

I was going thru my head about the phone calls, and I was getting a headache from all the possibilities involved. Thank goodness, Arley was coming to get me.

CHAPTER 37

Captain Fernandez was heading my way, looking none too happy.

"What's up, Cap, what can I help you with?"

"Okay, here is the deal, no one is to leave the premises. All the relatives and interested parties have been notified, so this place is going to be full of folks, so we better get ready for a cluster-fuck of people wanting answers. My deputies are out on a search and rescue in the Glades, so I am shorthanded, and I would appreciate you being my eyes and ears, as long as you play by the book, and don't try to be a nuisance."

"Moi, a nuisance? Heaven forbid, count me in."

"Seriously, it is going to get crowded here with the FBI coming, probably someone from the Bureau of Indian Affairs, in addition to the relatives."

"What relatives are coming?

"The relative is Gina's Father, who just so happened to have conveniently flown into Naples. I overheard Gina telling Powell about it. And, by the way, you are right, something is fishy here, can't put my finger on it though."

"Agreed, by the way, Cap'n, who has jurisdiction on this site?"

"Well, Jose, this is where it gets dicey, tribal laws do. But, if it is criminal in nature as this is, State and Feds can get involved, hence the upcoming cluster-fuck of agencies swinging their dicks to see who has the biggest."

I couldn't help but laugh. "Captain, at least you don't have to worry about having a dick to swing."

She laughed, too. "Oh, don't you worry, I might not have one, but I can swing it with the best of them. I didn't make Sergeant at Beach P.D. or Captain here, without having a set of brass ovaries. By the way, stop calling me Captain when there's no one around."

I liked her, she was straight, and to the point. I saluted her and bowed.

"Geezus, you are a horse's ass. By the way, did your contact find out anything?"

"Yes, indeed, my dear. And I hope this gets me an honorary Tribal police badge after this. It seems Steve got a call first from a private dick in Tampa, then Gina received a call from a phone registered to an LLC in Saint Lucia, and the third call was generated from the burner phone, don't know from who or to whom at this point. Burners are hard to trace, as you know."

"Fat chance on getting that badge Castillo. I have enough jackasses on my staff, don't need another, this is already a shit show, getting interesting to say the least."

"Yep, glad we have a little time waiting for everyone to show up, I need time to think this thru."

"You and me, Cubano, we have a lot of shit to sift thru, how about a cold one?"

"Never thought you'd ask, you don't have anything stronger, do you?"

"There's that captain shit again, call me Arley, please. And, no, my bottle of Havana Rum is back at my desk."

"Got it, cold one it is. I think this is going to be the beginning of a wonderful relationship."

"In your dreams son, in your dreams. I like the Casablanca reference though."

"Damn, that's twice I've heard that this week."

"Someone else said that to you, n your dreams, imagine that what a shock. Let's go before the circus gets here."

There was a helicopter heading in, we saw it land, and saw the Casino logo on it.

"What now?" Arley's asked.

"So sorry I forgot to mention that I called John Bond from the casino to give him an update."

She looked at me with fire in her eyes. "You know, Castillo, you could give a girl a heads up."

"After all the info I have received, my head is about to explode, my apologies."

"Anything else you want to share with me?" Arley was trying to stay calm.

Arley introduced herself to Bond and brought him up to date. He had a lackey with him, who Bond introduced as Stanley Milkey, Legal affairs for the Casino. He reminded me of a weasel, no other way to put it.

Bond turned to me, with a not-too-happy look on his face. "Castillo, I hope this mess can be squared away with no harm to the Casino's reputation. We hired you to keep an eye on them, and they appeared to have ducked your surveillance."

"As you will see in a bit, there was a concerted effort by parties to get them out without anyone's knowledge. Be patient, it will all come out soon we're just waiting for everyone to get here."

Arley took the opportunity to chime in. "Mr. Bond, please head inside. It shouldn't be too much longer before we start."

When we got back to the office, I called the number that Jim had gotten me from Steve's phone. It was Guardian Investigations in Tampa, and the recording said to leave a message, and they would get back to me shortly.

Ten minutes later, my phone rang, but did not show an incoming number. I answered it, anyway.

"Castle Investigations, how may I help you?"

"What the hell does a P.I. from Miami want to do with me?" A gruff voice no doubt, like they were gargling with rocks.

I put on my best British accent. "Is that anyway to speak to a fellow gumshoe, mate?"

"Judas H Priest, man, get to it. I don't have time for celebrity investigators."

"Ah, that is why you took ten minutes to call me; you did a Google search on my number, and you must have graduated at the top of your class, at private dick school."

There was silence and heavy breathing, coming from the other end.

"Okay, dipshit. You have one minute, or this call is over."

"What did Steve Osceola hire you for?"

More silence, more heavy breathing.

"None of your business, you know better than to ask me that. If you had graduated at the top of your class, you'd know he's my client, my case."

"He is my case, too. Lots of folks were paid to watch him."

"Is that right? I was not paid to watch him; he needed me to watch someone for him."

"Care to tell me about it?"

"Not a chance, again you should know better."

I decided to get right to it. "Steve is dead, care to trade info now?"

"Holy Mother of God! What the fuck?"

"Hope I have your attention now."

"You do, I'm Sam Larson, by the way. So, guess we'll have an information exchange. Here's the deal: Steve wanted me to go to the poker room at the casino, and play poker when Gina was working. He wanted me to see if there were any players that Gina treated differently than the others. It took me a while, but I noticed two fellows that appeared to be giving her napkins with something written on them."

My curiosity was peaked. "Can you describe these so-called fellows?"

"Sure, it's really easy to do. One fellow reminded me of a peacock, colorful clothes and hair that stood straight up. The other fellow was a stereotypical grease ball, slicked back hair, chomping on a cigar, rough looking character."

Man-o-man, my spidey sense was on alert now.

"Tell you what, Sam, you know where the Big Cypress reservation is located at?"

"Sure, been there a few times, why?"

"Why don't you head on down here, the body is still warm, there's lots going on, and another set of eyes that are involved in this couldn't hurt."

"Sure, I happen to be headed there, anyway. I talked to Steve, not too long ago, and he wanted me to show up there, said he would tell me why when I arrived."

"Great, see you soon." I'll be damned; my head was really going to explode.

I knew it was going to be a long night.

CHAPTER 38

It was an interesting group that was slowly gathering at the reservation. Jones and Powell were representing the Tribe, Arley representing the Tribe's law enforcement. John Bond and the corporate attorney representing the Casino, a low-level lackey from the Bureau of Land Management, who was so new that she did not have a business card made yet. She introduced herself as Molly Moreno. Papa Esposito called his daughter and said he would be arriving shortly.

Coffee had been brewed, water bottles had been laid out, and Arley had cordoned off around the crime scene with tape. She mentioned that the forensic team was running late, due to a large crime scene in Naples, and the on-call FBI agent was with them.

I was outside, standing next to Arley, when a vehicle pulled up, and a tall blonde woman stepped out of it wearing sweatpants, a sweatshirt, and running shoes. She had her hair in a ponytail, and looked like she came straight from the gym.

Arley sighed. "Oh shit, here comes Miss tight ass herself, heard of her, get ready."

She walked right up to Arley, as she was hanging her badge on a chain around her neck. "You in charge here? I'm Missy Royce, Florida Department of Law Enforcement."

"Yes, Arley Fernandez, Tribal police. As you can see, we have a homicide here waiting for forensics to show up, it seems to be a stand your ground situation, and are waiting for an attorney for the shooter to show up, as she has requested one to be present before we go any further. I did talk to her before she lawyered up and said that she and her boyfriend had an argument, did not say what it was about, and he pulled on her, and she reacted."

Missy was tapping her foot and appeared deep in thought. "Hell's bells, this is going to be a territorial clusterfuck. I'm going to call my boss to see who has the jurisdictional rights here. Who is this guy?" She pointed right at me.

I stuck my hand out for a shake. "Jose Castillo, Joe Castle Investigations, pleasure to meet you."

She stuck her hand out, and pulled back right away, and gave me a hard stare. "I've head of you from my colleagues in Miami. You are loose cannon, with no regard for protocol."

"You know my reputation of being a jackass is intact, making waves." I couldn't resist.

She chuckled. "Oh yeah, a jackass that's full of himself. What's your play here, Castillo?"

"I was hired by the Casino to keep an eye on the couple, who both worked there. Gina Esposito is a high stakes poker hostess. Steve Osceola was a pit boss, that's him lying on the ground over there."

"Osceola? Fuck me, and the horse I rode in on! This really is a clusterfuck, be back, I'm going to call my boss."

Arley looked at me and smiled. "Ain't she just peachy?"

"Damn, she's wound up tighter than a junkie on an eight-ball."

We both laughed quietly, as two cars pulled up. Two men got out of one car: a large older man who had trouble moving, who I assumed to be Esposito. The other man was younger, and had bodyguard written all over him, and he was wearing a leather jacket.

The other man, who was alone, was tall and lanky. He moved our way, with a languid stride. I assumed that was Sam. He got to us first, as Esposito was using a cane and taking his time.

"Castillo? Sam here, pleasure to meet you."

Arley looked at me. "Okay, another thing you forgot to tell me about, divulge please."

"I invited him, he was asked by Steve to look into something relating to Gina, figured it could not hurt."

"Great, more people involved, what fun." She turned to Sam. "Captain Fernandez, Tribal police. I am currently in charge here for the moment anyway."

Sam shook her hand. "Sam Larson, my pleasure Ma'am, just trying to help out here."

"Call me Ma'am one more time, and I will take you on a tour of the alligator pond we have out back."

"Sorry Ma'am, I mean Captain, just brought up to treat people properly."

"No sweat, anything you care to add to this shit-show?"

"If you don't mind, I will talk to Castillo first, and see if what I know is relevant."

"Okay, for the moment, but I will need a statement from you if it affects this case. See you two inside, the gang is all here." She headed to the office, with a full head of steam.

CHAPTER 39

Sam told me what he found out about Gina, and I decided to keep that information to see how things were going to play out.

Esposito finally hobbled up to us. "Who the hell are you? And where is my daughter?"

This was going to be fun. Esposito was about five feet tall, easily two-hundred and fifty pounds, and he reminded me of Danny DeVito. His associate was what I call a "twitcher" herky-jerky movements he couldn't stay still if he tried.

"I am Jose Castillo and I'm a private eye who was hired by the Casino to keep an eye on Gina and Steve. This is Sam Larson who was hired by Steve to look into something pertaining to Gina. Who is your associate?"

"This is my attorney, Lou Vilardo who is here to protect Gina. So, you two are just private dicks, ha! I will go in and speak to whoever is in charge, you too are just chumps."

"Well, nice to meet you too Pops, an attorney, huh? I thought he was your bodyguard, what law school did he graduate from? Vinnie Boom-bats University? And, by the way, ditch the tough guy leather jacket, this is Florida, the humidity will kick in shortly, and you'll think you are wrapped in a condom inside a cannoli shell, baking in the oven."

Esposito got right up in my face, and he was as red as a plum tomato.

"Listen, you wetback motherfucker! You don't mess with me or..."

I interrupted him. "Or I'll be swimming with the fishes, wearing cement shoes? Come on, Pops, lighten up. Besides, I'm not Mexican, even though some of my brethren came over from Cuba on rafts to get away from communism."

Lou was balling his fists, and he looked like he was going to jump right out of his shoes. "Come on, Uncle. Let's go inside, before I get nasty."

"Louis, you take one step my way, and you are going to need a dental surgeon, an orthopedic surgeon, bailing wire, and you'll be wearing a diaper for a month once they put you together." I had shifted sideways to make less of a target. I noticed Sam had shifted sideways, too.

Esposito blinked a couple of times and backed up. "Come on, Lou. Let's go help Gina, fuck this Cuban cockroach, and Lurch." They headed to the office, as best as Pops could wobble.

Sam looked at me. "Lurch, Lurch? I haven't heard that since high school."

"Shit my man, I haven't heard Cuban cockroach since a few days ago."

I gave Sam an idea of what I had in mind, and he agreed to go along with it.

CHAPTER 40

We were getting ready to head to the office, when we saw Missy jogging back over to us, so we waited for her. She was athletic, and certainly worked out often from the look of her chassis.

"Getting in the workout you're missing out on, young lady?"

"I've got to get it when I can. When I am not out in the field, I am usually filling out reports."

"Hey, this is Sam Larson, he's a private investigator who I think might have something relating to the case, I asked him to join us."

"The more the merrier. Missy Royce, FDLE, nice to meet you." They shook hands, and I could tell there was a bit of a spark there between them, you never know.

We went to the office, and everyone had taken up a territory: Esposito, Gina, and Lou were in one corner with Jones and Powell next to them. Arley and Molly, from the Bureau of Land Management, were over by the coffee maker, John Bond and his lackey were sitting at the table.

Arley walked to the head of the table and sat down. "Okay everyone, take a seat, and let's see if we can figure this out."

I sat to Arley's left, Sam next to me, to Arley's right were Missy and Molly. Next to them were the two Casino reps.

Arley cleared her throat and placed both hands on the table. "No one is being charged right now, but I do have the right to postpone any charges, until all the facts are clear. There seems to be a lot of interested parties involved, which will make things a bit more complicated, but I will make sure all parties have their two cents worth in the matter."

Lou spoke up. "Has Gina been read her Miranda rights?"

"No, she has not, because she has not been charged with anything. Now, please, can everyone introduce themselves, so we know who we are? I am Arley Fernandez, Tribal police captain."

Missy and Molly identified themselves, and their respective positions and duties in their organizations. Molly looked like she did not want to be involved.

When it was Gina's turn, she was sniffling, and did not even look up. She just said morosely: "Everyone knows who I am."

Lou introduced himself as Louis Vilardo, Esquire representing Miss Gina Esposito on behalf of her father, Giancarlo Esposito.

Esposito was next, and he gruffly introduced himself, and said he was a wholesaler from Brooklyn.

The Casino representatives were as droll and plain as you could imagine corporate lawyers to be, even in spite of their three-thousand-dollar suits.

Powell and Jones introduced themselves as elders of the Tribe and spoke of their intensions to protect the Tribe's interests.

Sam was next, most of them did not know who he was.

He clasped his hands in front of him and looked around the table. "My name is Samuel Larson. I am a private investigator who was hired by Steve Osceola three months ago to look into a suspicion he had about Gina Esposito."

Everyone at the table perked up, all were paying rapt attention to Sam.

Esposito glared at Sam. "You'd better be careful what you say about my girl, or my lawyer here will sue you for slander." He pointed to Lou, who tried to duplicate Esposito's glare, but didn't have the meanness in him that his uncle had acquired over years.

Sam glared right back at Esposito. "Just doing my job with no preconceptions, I was asked by Mister Osceola to become a regular at the high stakes poker room, and to just observe Gina's interactions with the players, and to see if there was anything out of the norm."

Esposito looked at Gina. "What the fuck, he didn't trust you?"

Gina never looked up but answered. "No daddy, I was never unfaithful to him."

"Then, what the fuck was going on?" He looked back at Sam. "Go ahead, carry on, this better be on the up and up, or I'll make sure your P.I. license is pulled, you capiche?"

Sam nodded at Esposito. "Got it, loud and clear, I will continue. So, after months of going to the poker room a few times a week, I noticed that Gina was paying particular attention to a man who had an accent from the Baltic States, had heavily tattooed arms, and instead of tipping her with poker chips, like most poker players do, he would tip her with one-hundred dollar bills."

To say that the table had Sam's rapt attention was an understatement.

Sam continued. "Once when I was sitting next to this man at the table, I noticed in the process of tipping Gina with the one-hundred-dollar bill, that there was either a business card, or a piece of paper in the folded bill."

The two casino reps were staring at Gina, and the lawyer type excused himself from the group, he said he would be stepping outside, no doubt to make a call.

Lou spoke up. "So, what? That doesn't mean a hill of beans, a paper? a note, a business card? No laws broken there."

I wondered what law school Lou had graduated from, and what his closing argument in class would have been like.

Sam kept on going. "Being an experienced investigator, with me having to testify in court many times I know that, so I knew I needed a little more information to paint a better picture. I followed the tattooed man when he was leaving and wrote down the license plate of the car the valet brought up for him. I used my contact at DMV to find the car was registered to an LLC in St. Lucia, which after peeling back a few layers of ownership, I discovered a holding company based in North Miami leased the car, and that the corporate address was a post office box, belonging to a day spa in Miami Beach."

There was a sudden flurry of activity: Missy and Molly were making notes on their phones, John Bond from the casino excused himself and stepped outside, Lou was whispering something to Esposito, Jones and Powell were talking to each other.

Suddenly, the forensic team entered the room asking for Arley, and a man that was trailing the team went straight to the coffee station and poured himself a cup.

If he was the FBI agent, he certainly did not look the part, his suit was disheveled, his shirt was wrinkled, he had on a bolo tie, and he looked like he hadn't slept in days. His gray hair was a mess, and he had a droopy mustache that was unkempt to say the least. The only thing on him that was clean were his snakeskin cowboy boots, with silver toe tips that gleamed.

The forensic team finished talking to Arley, and said they were going to work on the scene, and they would be reporting back to her when they were finished.

The agent sauntered over to Arley, and produced his ID. He pulled up a chair, turned it around, and straddled it. Then, he laid his coffee cup on the table, and rested his arms on the chair's back.

"Howdy Ma'am, you look like you are in charge here. Billy Bob Hoskins, Federal Bureau of Investigation, Orlando to Key West, saw the body outside. Anything I can do?" He appeared disinterested, but you could tell by his eyes that he did not miss much.

Arley held her hands up. "Not much at the moment, Agent Hoskins, but things are headed in a weird direction if you want to stick around. I've heard of you, a legend at the bureau, the only agent that does what he wants, dresses like he wants, and based on your track record you always get your man."

"Well, Miss, I appreciate the compliment. I'm getting by on reputation nowadays, half the perps I go after are women and most of the crimes are electronic, digital or software based. So, I am like a caveman hunting for dinosaurs that do not exist anymore. I'm too old to learn this computer horseshit, only reason I'm still working is because I asked for a transfer to a warm weather location, and surprisingly they gave it to me, only two more years till I retire. And please call me Billy Bob if you will, I feel old enough around you youngsters, no need to be called Mister."

"Consider it done, Billy Bob. If you need a break, you can use my office next door, if you so desire."

"Much obliged, Miss. Who is this guy next to you? He has been scrutinizing me without saying a word, since I sat down, bet he's a private dick, or ex-cop, or something."

"Good call on all counts, agent. Jose Castillo, former cop, now a private investigator, at your service." I stuck out my hand; his grip was a lot stronger than I thought it would be.

"Yep, kinda figured, believe I have heard of you from LEO's down South; bit of an ass, full of yourself, but you are a straight shooter and get results, left Metro-Dade because you wouldn't play politics. And you did not agree with plea bargains on your collars that prosecutors would use to clear and lighten their case load."

Damn, this guy was thorough, and knew his territory. "Holy shit, Bob, you are a walking font of information, nice to meet you. Think I heard my buddy, Nate Devine, at Metro singing your praises once."

"Nate? Just one time? That ol' son of a bitch, give him my best. Another good guy, of the few down that a way. He can play the political game, that's why he's lasted so long."

Arley cleared her throat. "Now, that you boys are done with old home week, and the mutual admiration society, let's get everybody the fuck back here, and see if we can figure this shit out."

Billy Bob slapped his thigh and looked at me. "Gawd damn, she's a cop, she's cute, she curses, and she's spunky. I got daughters older than her, if not I'd buy her a steak dinner."

Arley laughed. "Bob, you are showing your age. First, I can buy my own dinner, and I wouldn't eat a steak, I don't want to die early from a coronary embolism, and its lobster for me thanks. Let's put a bow on this baby, and let's call it a day."

I had a plan in mind, it was murky, some guessing would be involved, but I hoped it would help me to get to the bottom of this mess.

CHAPTER 41

The plan was starting to take shape. Mustafa had made the five vest bombs, and six remote controlled explosive devices. The van and the dirt bikes had been purchased, fueled and stashed behind their rental home.

The men had received a message from Aaron, that he would be visiting them later that day, and they were starting to get excited.

Mustafa had fitted the vests on all of them and made the necessary adjustments. Fadi and Malik had been taking helicopter flight lessons at a school which was situated on the Palm Beach County Sheriff's aviation department's location.

Young Fadi was pacing in the living room, like a caged tiger. "Why can't Aaron just send us the plan in an encrypted email, so we can start going over it?"

Mustafa, being the oldest, placed his hands on Fadi's shoulders. "Do not be so impatient, young Fadi. There are many things that have been put in motion by others that have taken months, if not years on this plan. Who knows how much money has been spent on us, and things we cannot even begin to understand? Be patient, think of how many years we have been at this, and we are only days away from executing revenge on those who have sacrificed our loved ones."

Fadi took Mustafa's hands of his shoulders and stepped back. "Sacrificed? Any more than we have already? Five years of our life, missing our families, living like monks!"

Sitting in the corner inspecting his vest, Bahir looked up, and pointed at Fadi. "Do not forget those who have died for our cause, do not forget those who lost a loved one or entire families to cowardly drone pilots, sitting behind a computer screen squeezing a trigger, releasing a drone bomb from safe haven." Bahir pointed at his vest. "Don't forget the hundreds of our brethren who have worn vests like this one, without thinking twice about it. That, my young friend, is real sacrifice."

All their phones chirped at once. Aasif had his phone next to him. "It's Aaron, he wants us to step outside, and to leave our phones at home."

They stepped outside to find a small old school bus parked in front of their home, with Aaron at the wheel waving them aboard. They settled in, and Aaron closed the door and headed West.

Mustafa was first to speak. "Brother Aaron, why the old school bus? And where are we going?"

"I borrowed it from one of our mosques in Fort Lauderdale. That way, I did not have to rent a vehicle, leaving a paper trail, and it being an old bus it does not have technology like GPS, which can be tracked and traced."

"Well thought out, my brother, where are we headed?"

"I am taking you on a tour where you will be going, all within a short distance and explain on the way. Since we are all together, there are no electronics on board, and nothing will be in writing. I will be sending each of you separate instructions, and you only can retrieve it with the code I will send you. And, yes, it is the site we have used before, it is encrypted, and once you read the instructions they will disappear."

Fadi, who had a nervous twitch in his leg, spoke up. "Finally! It's time to get this done, I cannot wait."

Aaron raised a hand. "There is great reward, only for those among us, who are patient with the decree of their Lord, young Fadi."

"*Inshallah, Ameen.*" was repeated by all the men.

"Yes, indeed, my brothers. We will be overseen by our God, the route we are taking will be reversed on the Day of Judgment. Number one will be leaving his country club, there is only one way to get to his mansion in Palm Beach, the Southern Boulevard crossover on I-95 will be where we will strike. As you will see, our plan will only allow for that, since Bahir will create a distraction with the van on I-95, the authorities will not attempt side roads, since the focus on protection will be mainly on Southern Boulevard."

"It's about time!" Fadi was literally bouncing on the seat.

Mustafa spoke up. "Won't they have snipers on the rooftops?"

"Of course, they will, but their arrogance of looking for a lone gunman will backfire on them. They will not be prepared for a coordinated attack, and the intensity of your attack should temporarily buy you some time." Aaron had turned the bus into the parking lot of the Summit Boulevard Library, which was across the street from the only entrance and exit to the Presidents country club.

Fadi's nervous twitch was increasing in intensity. "What do you mean by buying only some of us some time, not all of us?"

Aaron had parked the bus, facing the country club's entrance. "Dear Fadi, some of you will be exposed, some will not. Besides, we all signed up to be martyrs, eventually entering Paradise, and getting our heavenly rewards."

Fadi was sweating profusely. "We? What do you mean "we"? You mean us? Isn't your involvement only as a facilitator?"

"You do not know what I will do as part of this operation. One thing is for sure; I will not be captured and interrogated by the authorities. I will gladly take my life before they get their hands on me."

Aasif cleared his throat. "Fadi, if you have any doubts about our mission, we need to know now, there can be no room for error."

Fadi stood up and continued his nervous twitch. "I am not doubtful of our intent, I am just impatient, and want to get this over and done with."

"I understand, young man. After all this time, you must be yearning to do what all of you were fated to do. Be patient, the day is upon us, we will prevail." Aaron voice was a smooth, as it was calming. He hugged Fadi, who started to weep.

Fadi tried to break away from Aaron to no avail. "I know you are scared and impatient but think of what this team will accomplish with you as part of it. We could do it without you but think of the effort you have put into this mission."

Aaron let Fadi go. Fadi rubbed his eyes and looked at the entire team. "I'm not scared, I just want to finish this, and I'm so tired of waiting."

"Just a few more days, my brother, just think how long it has taken us to get to this point. I will drive you all back, and your instructions will be sent to you, by the time we get you home."

On the way back, which was by way of Southern Boulevard eastbound, Aaron pointed out the Australian Avenue exit, the Hilton hotel on the Northwest corner of Southern and I-95, and the Palm Beach Zoo on the Southeast corner.

When they reached the rental home, Aaron came in with them, and asked them to take a seat.

"Gentlemen, tie up all your loose ends, ask for a day off when we give you the date, or call in sick, whatever you need to do, pay rent and utilities ahead of time, and burn any papers you have. Wipe all the memory in your electronics, then donate your computers and I-pads to the different Goodwill stores, along with all your clothes. Buy some acid, and put your burner phones in it, after you take the Sim cards out, and burn those separately."

Malik, who had not said much, spoke up. "Thank you, brother Aaron, for your devotion to our cause, Allah be with you, I have faith that all will work out in our favor."

Aaron shook all their hands, in addition to an embrace. "*Allahu Akbar!* My brothers in arms, be swift, be precise, wield that tip of the spear proudly, and be well."

After Aaron left, they all went to their computers and I-pads to read their instructions. There was a whoop, and a loud yes was heard from Fadi's room.

CHAPTER 42

Arley was rounding up everyone, back in when I received a call from Tracy. "Okay, boyo, here is the delivery timetable I put together, after viewing the CCTV tape you sent me from their front door: the pizza was delivered first, who do think they buy their restaurant supplies from? If you guessed a company owned by Papa Esposito, you win. There's the Uber Eats delivery, which the couple did order after all. The flowers came last, and what's funny is that there was no record of a Door Dash order, even though one of the neighbors remembered seeing a car with their logo in the parking lot, and I was told a Door Dash driver lives in the complex.

"Curiouser and curiouser, who delivered the flowers, then? Our friend from the Baltic's must have taken the flowers to his room, put the bomb in it, and had it delivered."

"I saw a man deliver them on the tape; I'm assuming he was from a courier service. Following up on that, as we speak, he shouldn't get too far, he could hardly walk."

"Did you say he could hardly walk? Describe him to me."

"Say, mid-seventies past eighty, walked with a gait, frail you could say."

My mind was racing. "Tracy, do me a great favor, get to the flower shop and stake it out. If the delivery man there is the same one, then tail him, and find out where he lives. His name is Arthur Meyer, don't do anything until I get back."

"Is he a bad man involved in all this?"

"I don't think so, but it's too coincidental. Now, what did you find out?"

"Well Jose, I did a bit of snooping, and there was a way for them to get out unseen. There is a trash chute on every floor, then being on the second floor, it would have been a small drop into the dumpster, then out the garbage room. Your CCTV tape showed them headed that way with trash bags, remember? But they never came back."

"A desperate move. I wonder how they were warned."

"The flowers must have been what tipped them off, they must have moved fast, and I am thinking the bomb was on a timer not on a remote. Thanks, you've been a big help, gotta go."

I think I was getting an idea of what happened, now to piece it together.

Everyone had come back in the room, and took their seats, except Billy Bob. He stood by the coffee station nursing his cup of coffee.

I pulled Arley to a corner. "I know you don't know me from Adam, but I think I have most of this figured out. I am going to ask you to trust me, you've heard that I can be a jerk sometimes and full of myself, but you also heard that I do the right thing. I am incorruptible, I believe in justice, please just trust me and let me get started, work with me here, I think you'll catch on fast."

"What? Did I miss something?" Arley looked concerned.

"No, Captain, you probably would have figured it out in time, but I think outside the box. I have to catch them off-guard. There is a set of men's golf clubs in the back of the Jeep, left-handed clubs. I looked at Steve's left hand in which he did not have a gun, he was holding the gun in his right hand. He had calluses on his left hand and his watch is on his right hand where most lefties wear them. There's a pretty good chance he is left-handed, why would he hold a gun in his right hand?"

"Holy fuck Jose, you might be onto something there, that's what you looked at when you dropped your keys by Steve, clever. So, she shot him on purpose, what if he isn't left-handed?"

"I have a fifty-fifty chance of being right. Hey, one day I might be in the gumshoe hall of fame, eh?"

"Still full of yourself, but I'll give you credit for that, again, very clever. I feel this is going to be a strange one, hang tight I might need some more of that out-of-the-box thinking."

"I'm going to need that burner phone, do you still have it?" My fingers were crossed.

She reached into her shirt pocket. "Here it is, hope you know what the fuck you are doing."

"Damn, glad you kept it as evidence. This might unlock everything, thanks."

I noticed everyone was watching us, all of them were waiting for us to enter, it was going to be a bumpy night.

Arley walked to her chair at the head of the table. "Okay folks, have a seat, it's showtime."

CHAPTER 43

Arley cleared her throat. "Okay people, this is going to be a fact-finding mission, no one at the moment is under any scrutiny. I just want to know how everyone is tied to Gina and Steve, what contacts might have been between some of you and the couple? No one is pressured to say anything they do not want to, you are not under oath, but if any evidence or connections that are discovered thru this process, there are enough law enforcement agencies represented here, that I cannot guarantee repercussions from them if they should decide a law has been broken. So, choose your words and actions carefully, also anyone is free to leave if you chose to."

Esposito jabbed his nephew Louis in the ribs, Louis spoke up. "Officer, if we are free to leave, then I would like to take Gina and her father away from here, this is upsetting both of them."

Billy Bob chuckled, quietly. I looked at him and smiled.

Arley twirled a pen she had in her hand and looked at Louis. "First of all, it's Captain Fernandez, not officer. Second, anyone can leave anytime they want, except Gina, she is the focus of what is going on."

Louis jumped out of his seat. "You can't keep her here, unless you charge her, that's the law."

"Mister Vilardo, whatever you saw on Law and Order on the television will not work here. We have laws that are bit different than the outside world, sit down and wait for everything to come out. If indeed it was truly in self-defense, Gina will be free to go. Forensics is working outside, and we are working in here, the truth will come out one way or another. Sit down and, unless you have a valid point, do not interrupt again."

"I have a law degree from NYU, I'll have you know." Vilardo sat down and puffed his chest out like a peacock.

Arley placed her hands on the table and looked at everyone. "I am going to repeat what I was told by Gina and the Elders about what transpired, in order to bring everyone up to speed. If anyone does not agree with my statement just raise your hand, and we will tackle every comment like civilized folk. I will have Jose Castillo jump in with some information, since he was hired by the Casino to check up on the couple, to make sure there were no HR rules being broken."

This caused some people to stir in their seats. Sam Jones, Lou Vilardo, and John Bond, all raised their hands at the same time.

Arley pointed to Sam. "Go ahead, Sam, what is your question?"

"What were Gina and Steve under suspicion for?'

"Mister Bond, you had a hand up, answer his question, and then your comment can follow." Arley was making sure she was controlling the room.

Bond put his hands together, hesitated for a moment, like he was measuring his words. "Well, by answering Mister Jones, I will make the comment I wanted to in the first place. First, we prefer to not have our employees get involved with each other, especially if they did not have a previous relationship, and especially if they work in the same area. If, for example, one of them works in food service, and one in the game room, we usually look the other way. As you know, we have surveillance cameras everywhere, and our Security Director brought to our attention that Miss Esposito had more than a few interactions with a certain gentleman, who was on our radar. That is why we requested Mister Castillo to do surveillance on the couple."

Missy Royce from FDLE did not raise her hand, she just jumped in. "Could you elaborate on what you meant by radar, Mister Bond?"

Vilardo jumped up. "I had my hand up, I was next!"

"You'll get an opportunity, now please sit back down." Arley was getting aggravated with him.

"Certainly, Ms. Royce. Within certain parameters of proprietary security programs that I cannot divulge, obviously we have client information on their membership application, but we do an extensive background check on members that meet certain criteria, which I am not at liberty to divulge."

Missy continued to poke Bond. "So, certain members are looked at a little harder, if they have red flags according to your criteria. Might that mean a criminal background?"

Bond was slicker than owl shit. "Ms. Royce, you can come up with your own conclusions, but you can surmise what might or not constitute a red flag."

"So as long as you are not violating any Amendment rights, Mister Bond." If Missy was grating on Bond's nerves, he did not show it.

Vilardo stood up. "That's what I wanted to comment on, I want to make sure Gina did not have her Fifth Amendment rights violated."

Agent Hoskins covered his face with his hand. "Oh, boy" he murmured.

Arley had enough. "Mister Vilardo if you cannot stay seated, I will handcuff you to your chair, got it? I will continue, so the story is that the couple contacted Mister Powell after the incident at their apartment and requested refuge at the reservation. Upon their arrival, there was an argument between the couple. And, according to Gina and Mister Jones who were the only witnesses to this, Steve pulled a gun on her, and she in turn shot Steve. Is that correct, Miss Esposito?"

Gina was still not looking up. "Yes, that's what happened, Mister Jones verified that."

"Indeed, he did, so noted." Arley turned to me. "Mister Castillo, please proceed carefully."

I was flying by the seat of my pants. "Okay folks, bear with me here, this story will have a lot of moving parts, I have some facts and some opinions and conjecture. The facts are based on information gained back in Tampa, and the deliveries made to their apartment, as well as phone records of those involved."

At that point, Gina looked at me, at Powell, then at Vilardo, it was the thing that caused Vilardo to speak up.

Vilardo stayed seated for a change. "I'm going on record that this is just a fishing expedition. And, this man, Castillo, is not a law officer, his comments have no validity here."

Arley stared at Vilardo. "Noted, but please keep in mind evidence gathering is what we are doing here, so any information, no matter who it comes from, will be taken into account. Please, carry on Mister Castillo."

I proceeded carefully. "Based on our findings, the flowers delivered to the couple, which had a bomb in it, were purchased by a man who appeared to be of Russian descent, based on eyewitness testimony. Furthermore, based on that, his appearance indicated he might be involved with the Vory, which is a Russian criminal group. The pizza was delivered by a shop, far from the apartment, and it begs the question: why not a closer pizza parlor? An Uber order was also delivered to the apartment complex that the couple did order."

Papa Esposito spoke up. "What the hell does that have to do with any of this?"

"Mister Esposito, if you bear with me, you will see where this is headed. By the way, the pizza shop, that delivered to them just happens to buy their supplies from your company. Care to comment on that?"

If looks could kill, I'd be dead after the stare I got from Papa. Vilardo was next to address me. "Our company supplies thousands of restaurants, what's it to you?"

"It's just funny that there are three pizza shops closer to the couple, and one that your company has ties to just happened to deliver the pizza. My theory is, that Gina called her father with some concerns, and Papa had the pizza delivered, as a way of checking on the couple without arousing any suspicions."

Vilardo chuckled. "That's preposterous, you are grasping at straws!"

Arley looked at me a bit bewildered. "Get to the point Castillo, or else."

"Okay, here is where it gets a little clearer. I cannot say how I received this information, but Gina received a call from a spa in South Beach, which is tied to the Russians. Steve received a call from Sam Larson about his findings, all around the time they were headed here. There is a burner phone I have possession of, which was in Steve's console, which we will find out shortly who was called with it. I'm guessing Gina got in over her head with the Russians, and pulled out, hence the bomb sent to their apartment."

This caused a flurry of activity: Jones and Powell started whispering to each other, so did Bond and his lackey, Gina had her face in her hands, still crying, and Papa was consoling her. Missy and Molly excused themselves and were dialing their phone as they were walking out; Hoskins got up for another cup of coffee. Vilardo stood up again and was frantic. "I want to go on record again that this guy is not in law enforcement, and all of this could be lies."

Arley whispered to me: "You know you could give a girl a heads up."

"Trust me, there's more. I have a suspicion to who the phone call was made to, bear with me."

"Gawd Castillo, if this goes sideways, I'll be writing parking tickets again."

"You will be fine, I got this."

The ladies came back, the forensic team came in, pulled Arley to the side, and gave her a report.

Vilardo of course had to speak up, and he pointed at Arley. "Captain, I request you charge my client or release her, this is a sham investigation."

"I will do no such thing, everyone sit down, I will give Castillo a chance to finish."

"Finish what? This is a clown show!" Vilardo was going to blow a gasket.

Arley was going to blow one, too. "Sit down, dammit! For the last time, go ahead Castillo, and make it quick!"

I pulled out the burner phone, dialed the last number that was called. The phone that rang was Sam Jones.'

Jones reached in his pocket and turned it off. Everyone was looking at him. Powell, who was right next to him, gave him an incredulous look. Gina kept on weeping. Jones looked like he wanted to hide. But he spoke up. "I can explain, there's no harm in that call."

I raised my hand, "Here is my theory, and feel free to poke holes in it: Gina was contacted by the Russians to gain information on the Casino and Steve, since he was going to be the next Tribal Leader. The Casino is privately owned, and since they could not get their claws in that way, their method of operation is to be a supplier to a business, worm their way in, and gain leverage that way. But guess who supplies the Casino? That's right, her father's company. I'm guessing she played along with them to get information back to her father, so he could pre-empt any move by them. After she refused to continue to play ball with them, they decided to bomb their apartment. Also, they had a conduit to Steve thru her but, knowing the Russians, they probably had a backup plan, so it would not surprise me if you check Jones' phone, there are calls from South Beach on it."

"Captain, are you going to let this sham continue? This is speculation at best!" Vilardo was shouted.

"Yes, I am. He will finish, and I'll take it from there."

"Thank you, Captain. Now, Mister Larson was hired by Steve to keep an eye on Gina, and you have heard his report. He called Steve as they were making their way here, and you know by his description of the men that were passing notes to Gina, that they fit the profile of our Russian friends. Steve must have brought this up to her, and that is when the argument happened. I'm guessing Gina asked Steve to pull into a rest stop to use the bathroom, and she called Jones on the burner to tell him what Steve had discovered. Mister Powell, may I ask who was in the running for Tribal Leader?"

"It was a two-man race; Osceola and Jones." You could have heard a pin drop in the room.

"Were you here when the couple arrived?" I was feeling better about my theory.

"No, as a matter of fact. Jones asked me to get something from the other office for him."

"Thank you. So, the couple arrived, Jones was there to meet them, and he had a plan to get rid of Steve, used the story about the couple fighting, convincing Gina that was the only way to protect herself and her father's business. The bonus was that they already had an argument in the car. After Steve received the call from Larson, the mistake Jones made was putting the gun in Steve's right hand; he is left-handed, he has calluses on his left hand, he wears a watch on his right hand, like most lefties do, and there's a set of left handed clubs in his vehicle."

Hoskins looked at me, slightly nodded, and had on a small smile, which only I noticed.

Gina blurted out, while pointing at Jones: "He made me do it! I was so confused and upset, it happened so fast. I was scared and I didn't know what to do. I was trying to help my father, Steve was going to leave me, and tell everyone what I had done."

Papa started crying, and hugged his daughter, Vilardo patted her on the back, and Jones spoke up. "I request legal representation at this time."

Arley sighed, and read Gina and Jones their Miranda rights, then she handcuffed them. "I am charging Gina with manslaughter at this time, and Jones with accessory to murder. I am not a lawyer, but I am sure it will all come out in the wash, after the authorities get involved. Since said authorities are here, let's meet separately, and I will take your advice as per the charges, let's go to the back office." Arley, Missy and Molly headed that way.

Hoskins turned back towards me. "You know, Castillo, you have brass balls, good job. And, by the way, I'd like to know who gets your phone call information. I could use whoever it is from time to time. By the time I put in a request for a phone trace, the perps are usually gone before I can get a warrant."

"I'll check with him first, he's not too fond of the *Federales*, if you know what I mean."

"Well, you just told me he is a male, that's a fifty-fifty break right there."

Damn, he was good, he got me. We shook hands, and I said I hoped we would run into each other again.

"Oh, I am sure we will, especially since you are tight with Nate at Metro, he is a good guy, and I'll look both of you up next time I am in the area. Be well and stay out of trouble." He headed to the back room.

Powell had moved away from Jones and walked over to me. "I cannot thank you enough for your input. Please, bill me for your time, I will be happy to pay you."

"As I told you when you were in my office, I do not double bill. The Casino is paying me well, and I suppose there might be a bonus for me, after the smoke clears."

Powell shook my hand. "If there isn't one, let me know, you certainly deserve it."

"Thank you, I will. But I'm sure I won't take you up on your offer."

The four came out of the back room, Arley took charge. "Okay everyone, we are done here. We are good with the current charges and will let the legal system take over from here, appreciate your patience and cooperation."

Bond and his lackey came towards me, and Bond stuck out his hand. "Good job, Castillo. I had no idea this was going to be such a disaster when we hired you, but I am glad we did, send me your bill you certainly earned it."

FLORIDA CROSSING

"Sure thing ,will do. By the way, do you think I could get comped at your casino?"

"Oh, certainly, at all of them, consider it done." The weasel made a face after that.

"Thanks much, appreciate the hire, keep me in mind in the future."

Arley walked over to me. "Well, Castillo, you pulled it out of your ass, don't know how to thank you."

"No thanks needed, call on me if you need any help, take care of yourself, look me up if you come to Miami. Now, I got to wrap up with friends in Tampa, and then I have a golf tournament to go to."

"Golf, golf, seriously? You play that boring game?"

"I sure do, it keeps me humble."

"You humble? *No me jodas*, Cubano, let me know when that happens."

Little did I know that so-called boring game would put me right in the middle of an attempt on the life of the President.

CHAPTER 44

Once I got back to Tampa, I knew where to find Tracy and the Doughnuts, they were having a meal at the diner.

I brought them up to speed, and tried answering their questions as best as I could. Tracy needed more clarification.

Vinnie spoke up. "So, let me get this straight, Castillo. Gina got involved with the Russians, thinking she would be the go-between the Russians and her father, turn that info over to her father, so he could preempt any moves on their part. Steve had her watched because he didn't know what she was up to. Jones used their argument to his advantage to pit Gina against Steve and take him out of the running, and all of us were hired by interested parties who wanted to know what they were up to, is that about right?"

"That's about the gist of it, a tangled web for sure. By the way, Tracy, did you follow Meyer for me?"

"I sure did. Every afternoon, after he clocks out, he has one drink at a bar near the flower shop, just one drink and then he goes home, turns in for the night. Why did you want me to watch him?"

"I have a theory, which is a reach, so I want to talk to him before I leave town. Kids, it's been fun, you two watch your weight, I'm sure some widows might have an interest in you two, if you get in shape."

Vinnie spoke first. "Good Lord, Castillo, I get more pleasure out of food than a widow at this point."

Harry laughed. "Me too, at least the food doesn't talk back to me."

We all had a good laugh, said our goodbyes and I headed to see Meyer, hoping he was at his usual spot after work.

CHAPTER 45

Meyer was sitting at the end of the bar nursing a cocktail, I moseyed up and sat next to him.

He looked at me up and down, then said: "Look what the cat dragged in. What brings you into this sleazy bar, Castillo?"

"Arthur heard you wanted to see me. Two things: one, I want to buy you a drink for your help, and two, I want to run a theory by you, so that you can confirm or deny, no harm no foul here."

"Sure, I'll take you up on the drink, I can only afford one each day with my pension being what it is. As far as your theory, let's hear it."

I was going to be careful as I did not want to piss him off. "When we met, I got the impression you had some regrets in life about not doing the right thing, and not following your instincts, is that right?"

He looked at me with a solemn expression. "Go ahead, but tread carefully."

"I'm thinking you had a gut feeling about the Russian and the flower delivery, so you acted on it, because if something bad happened, you did not want to ignore your gut again."

The bartender came over, and I ordered whatever he was having for the both of us. Apparently, it was gin and tonic with Bombay.

He looked at me, put his hand on my shoulder, then said: "Carry on, that drink will buy you five more minutes, after that I am going home."

"So, here is my theory, somehow you managed to get yourself to talk to the Russian, when he was planning or going to deliver the flowers, and you convinced him to let you deliver them instead."

He took a healthy swig of his drink. "Carry on, so far so good there, Sherlock, you know I speak their language, that part was easy."

"Thanks, flying by the seat of my pants here, so bear with me. You probably convinced him it would be safer for you to make the delivery,

135

since that is your job anyway, and I bet you also told him it would be safe for him not being seen near the apartment."

"You are pretty good, carry on."

"Here it is: your instinct told you something was up, you took the flowers to them, probably felt the bouquet was heavier, saw or felt the bomb and you decided to warn the couple, did you not? You did not want to pass up a chance to do something good."

He looked me straight in the eyes. "Bingo! You are the next contestant on the *Price is Right*. If, and I really mean if, nothing had happened, I would have made an extra twenty bucks. But I followed my gut, glad I did, I knew something smelled funny, which is what I wanted to talk to you about, I didn't know if it was kosher to bring it up to you, not knowing whether you would turn on me. But, after reading up on you, you seem to want the scales of justice to balance no matter what the cost."

"Correct, good for you, Arthur. It took me a while to figure out why they left so fast but, since you were on my surveillance tape, I put two and two together, thanks for confirming it for me. So, there you have it, and if it feels any better, I agree with what you did, it was courageous of you holding a bomb not knowing when it would go off."

"Well, my Cuban friend, the Russian was insistent that I deliver it by a certain time, I don't need a reward, and just doing the right thing for a change is enough. If you think that is courageous, try slitting the throat of a concentration camp guard, so you can escape from pure hell. By the way, why did the Russians want to take them out?"

"They wanted to get their hooks in the casino one way or another, either thru Steve, being their supplier, or digging their hooks in his girlfriend Gina, simple as that. Okay, my friend if I can call you that, thanks again." I finished my drink.

"You may as long as I can call you the same, take care of yourself, stay away from the Russians, they bring nothing but trouble."

"I will, I'll try, got to run, I have a golf tournament to go to in Palm Beach."

Arthur laughed out loud. "Golf, shit, I've been playing for sixty years and haven't figured it out yet, don't get old my friend, good luck."

CHAPTER 46

The golf tournament was nothing out of the ordinary, money was raised for the Little Smiles organization, and the rumor was that the President's team was going to win no matter what. Sure enough, all the scorecards were turned in, except the President's team.

They waited to see what the lowest score was, before they turned in theirs, which just happened to beat our score by one stroke. That made our team come in second, so were invited to Marinlago for dinner and additional photo ops.

I told Glen I did not want to go to the President's home, but he told me that it would not look good on his office if I did not show. It would appear as an insult to the President, and the State Attorney's office could use all the political capital they could get with all the budget cuts, which had transpired in the last few years.

He knew I did not agree with the President's policies, and the way he had besmirched the office of the most powerful position on the planet, but he told me to buck up and to bite my tongue for a change, and to not cause any waves.

We had been pre-screened by the Secret Service. Teams had been required to supply player's names a month in advance of the golf tournament. I was surprised I had not been contacted by the authorities, due to my history of disdain for the man.

Our team gathered, and prior to entering one of the Secret Service vehicles for the short trip to Marinlago, we were given a "pep talk" by the agent in charge of our foursome, who everyone called Smitty. Just the basics: that our cell phones would be confiscated, to follow instructions regarding photo ops, no sudden moves, and anyone who needed to use the bathroom needed to inform the team handler, etcetera.

The caravan heading out consisted of six Secret Service vehicles; we were in the third car and the President was in the second one.

There were two motorcycle units in front of the caravan, and two in back. There was a helicopter overhead, four Palm Beach Sheriff vehicles behind the last motorcycle units, including a SWAT personnel carrier bringing up the rear.

We exited the golf course, made a left turn towards Congress Avenue, made a left on Congress, and headed north towards Southern Boulevard to catch the on-ramp. It should have taken less than ten minutes to arrive, since all intersections were being controlled by PBSO personnel.

It should have been a quick trip but, once we headed east on Southern and closing in on top of the I-95 overpass, all hell broke loose.

CHAPTER 47

Four of the men had received their post cards. Customers who had shown up at their place of work and were handed what looked like a small inspirational card, which said *Go in Peace*. Shortly, after receiving the card, there was a text on their phone that just had the number one on it.

Aasif was contacted the same way, two hours earlier. He knew what his instructions were, and he had been to the Summit Boulevard library, which was across the street from the President's country club, and he was able to watch the only gate to the club, where he could see the vehicles coming and going.

Earlier during the week, he had jogged a couple of times by the club entrance at night, and on the third night he got near the gates and was tying his shoelaces and took the opportunity to attach a Micro HD video camera using Velcro on top of one of the landscape lights, which lit the driveway.

This would, at the very least, give him a look towards the circular driveway, and he would have a heads up when things were starting to move. He was in the library, looking like he was reading a book, while looking at a live shot on his phone from the camera he had placed by the entrance. He had a backpack with him, which had the bomb vest in it, and all he had to do was jump on his dirt bike once the caravan started to move.

Bahir had taken the van they had bought, and his instructions were to go to the nearest Home Depot and pick up five daily workers that would sit around there waiting to be picked out for work. The plan was to head towards I-95 and Southern to create a diversion.

Mustafa had checked into the Hotel on the Northwest corner of I-95 and Southern a week earlier and had brought in at night an RPG-2 rocket propelled grenade launcher in a Bass case, so as to not attract any attention. He could not get the room he wanted, which faced the overpass, but he had scoured the building and had found a locked door to the roof, which he could easily break thru, and have a clear view of the area from there.

He had measured the distance to the overpass and had figured the maximum range he had with his weapon to be one hundred and sixty yards. He would have to shoot between the start of the ramp, and the center of the Interstate's overpass.

Fadi and Malik were at Beach Aviation adjacent to Palm Beach International airport, in their helicopter class. They had mentioned, when they started the class, that they were in EMT training, so when they showed up in EMT uniforms, no one was the wiser. The instructor had mentioned that there would be a no-fly zone at some point in the afternoon, while the President exited his golf course and headed to his home in Palm Beach, so flights would only be before or after that time. Timing would be everything, they had prayed that morning that all would go according to plan.

CHAPTER 48

Susan Schliff of FDLE met with PBSO sheriff Broadwater before they went into Bill Johnson's briefing.

"Hey, Rick, I know the Secret Service rarely pays attention to us locals, but I have a concern I want to run by you."

Broadwater had been in office for over twenty years and fended off every attempt to replace him by running an efficient office with a budget of over eight hundred million dollars, which taxpayers always brought up at election time. But Palm Beach County had never had a major incident during his tenure.

"Go ahead, Susan. We know we are just local peons, according to the swinging dicks from Washington, but run it by me anyway."

"Well, I know they will block all on and off ramps on Southern and 95, but there is no way to stop the traffic on 95, is there?"

"No, unfortunately, that would cause a major traffic issue. We get enough grief by closing the ramps, while the motorcade passes thru, even though it's for only ten minutes or so."

Susan decided to proceed anyway with her theory: "I did think about that. So, what is to stop anyone from stopping a vehicle on 95 under the overpass, and detonating a bomb?"

"Well, Susan, great minds think alike, so I will have two motorcycle officers on either side under the overpass, just sitting there watching."

She had to tread carefully here. "I thought of that, but if a vehicle comes to a sudden stop, how fast can your officers get to it, and stop a detonation?"

Broadwater looked at her sternly. "So, you are thinking I should have more officers stationed there, is that what you are getting at?"

"Yes, I do, you can never have enough personnel in that location. I think it's the weakest point."

"Thanks, Susan, you are right, I will triple the officers there. Let's go in and see what Bill and his team have planned."

They headed to the conference room, where Bill Johnson was already at the podium.

"Okay folks, it's showtime. In the next hour or so, the president's motorcade will be leaving the club, and head to his home thru Southern Boulevard. All birds, high altitude drones are in the air, Air and Marine operations are covering the Intracoastal and the ocean, and all video will be run thru the Big Pipe system, as some of you know but for those that do not it is a network of cameras that will feed all the video thru one centralized location, where we can look at real time mission data. Any questions?"

Sheriff Broadwater spoke up. "Bill, I am doubling down on personnel under I-95, Director Schliff and I came to the conclusion that more is good."

"Sounds good, Rick. Let's get him home safely, there's no chatter on the internet. But that's what worries me real terrorists don't blab their plans for the entire world, so all of us can see it. I'll remind you there was not a single manifesto posted from the 9-11 groups before their attack."

CHAPTER 49

Everything happens so fast in a situation like this that you do not know what is going on, and you feel helpless not knowing where the next blow is coming from, your head is on a swivel, trying to save yourself and those around you.

In the Army, our sniper team was always far from the action either on a rooftop or safe in the hills, and we rarely took on incoming rounds. Once, when we were fired upon by an RPG, my team was able to scramble in time to avoid any casualties.

I was sitting on the left rear seat, when I saw a trail of smoke out of my left eye, and my brain could not calculate what it was, until the RPG hit the second vehicle. In quick order, there were six explosions under us, and the whole bridge was shaking. The traffic on I-95 had come to a standstill, after the explosions, but I saw a white van on the shoulder of the highway heading towards the underpass at full speed.

There was chatter on the agent's radios saying "Code Red" over and over. I heard a motorcycle before I saw it jump over the side shoulder, and careen thru the air towards us, then a massive explosion came from it. I knew it was a suicide bomber, I knew this was a coordinated attack, and there would probably be more coming.

Our motorcade tried to speed up from the middle of the crossover, when it felt like an earthquake, and the majority of the overpass collapsed in front of us preventing our entire motorcade from moving forward. There was a swarm of agents around the President's vehicle with arms drawn; some were speaking into their mikes. All of a sudden, they started taking fire and some went down, the few that were not hit were pointing towards the hotel.

Glen and I managed to get out of our mangled vehicle, and I asked Smitty if help was on the way. He confirmed it, and suggested we get the hell out of there. I asked him if there were any long-range rifles on board. He nodded, and grabbed a Springfield M1a from our SUV and handed it to me. "I remember reading your file that you were in sniper school, do your thing, Castillo."

"I'm going to take out that sniper, if it's the last thing I do."

"Well, you better, he has our group pinned down. Help is on the way, but not fast enough for my taste."

Glen said he was going to check on the President, and carefully moved by the right side of our vehicle, knowing the shots were coming from the left.

I was familiar with the M1a, as it was my training rifle first year of sniper school. I took some deep breaths to calm myself, figuring I probably had one chance at taking the sniper out. I knew the M1a had a range of about a thousand yards, and I calculated the sniper to be about one-hundred and fifty yards, based on the muzzle flash I saw from the hotel's rooftop.

I saw Glen by the President's vehicle, he was talking to the President's detail, he pointed at the hotel, and then at me. They nodded when I raised my hand and spun it around, hoping they would get my drift, which was to create a diversion, hopefully causing the sniper to show himself.

The agent next to Glen spoke into his mike, and all of a sudden agents came out of the front car and headed towards the President's vehicle. Doors swung open in the vehicle, and there were bodies coming in and out of it.

I had taken my position, adjusted the scope, checked the wind, and breathed slowly. As soon as I saw the sniper's head pop out, I exhaled and gently squeezed the trigger. Bingo! His head exploded, like a watermelon at a Gallagher's concert. I still had it.

Sirens were coming from everywhere, and I heard the thump of helicopter blades, and saw a helicopter heading our way from the nearby airport. I assumed that was part of the help, I used the scope to look in the cockpit. I did not like what I saw: two young men who had scowls on their faces, so I went with my gut instinct and decided to take action.

I fired a shot at the cockpit but did not hit any of them. When I tried taking aim again, I heard the whoosh of a missiles, and by the time I squeezed the trigger, the helicopter was obliterated into a thousand pieces. Then, I saw an F-15 swinging by overhead, tilting its wings back and forth.

Sounds came over Scotty's earpiece, and he motioned us to follow him. We followed the President's details that were scurrying over the rubble toward the east side of 95. The President was surrounded, and Glen was trailing them.

Sheriff's vehicles were waiting for us on that side, along with West Palm Beach police, FDLE vehicles, and someone had brought along a personnel carrier for the ride.

It looked like the President was shoved into the personnel carrier, and before we were shoved into the trailing vehicle, we heard a scream coming from the side of the embankment, where there was a man was running up it towards us holding something in his hand, with a wire that ran into his shirt. He made it one step closer before he was turned into Swiss cheese by agent's fire. He must have had a device that self-detonated when released, because there was an immediate explosion sending shrapnel our way.

Luckily, he was fifty yards from us, so there were no casualties, just some minor shrapnel cuts. I was bleeding from my shoulder, and Glen was bleeding from his leg. I told Glen: "There goes our hope of joining the PGA Tour."

"Like we ever had a chance, eh Primo?"

We were laughing when Smitty rushed us into a nearby ambulance and pounded on the door for the driver to go. We had to wait for an EMT, who was pushed into the passenger's seat by two agents. His head was bandaged almost covering his entire head and most of his face. We appeared to be headed towards the President's estate, but the vehicle turned north on Olive Avenue. The driver turned to us, and said: "Boys, got instructions to take you to Good Samaritan hospital, hang in there, we have an escort!"

I saw two motorcycles in front with a Sheriff's SWAT truck and two motorcycles in the back with a black SUV that looked like the style the Secret Service use.

"Damn, I was looking forward to dinner and our second place trophies." I chuckled.

Glen looked at me and smiled. "You know, J.C., we are lucky to be alive, and all you can think about is dinner and a trophy!"

"Actually, I was looking forward to meeting his wife. I've seen her modeling pictures, and she is a fine specimen."

Glen shook his head. "Geezus, food, sports, and broads. Is that all you think about?"

"Nah, a good bottle of rum, too."

CHAPTER 50

Aasif left the library and had already mapped out a course that would take him away from the motorcade but would eventually catch up to it from a side road. He had procured a street version of a dirt bike, so he could ride either on or off-road. He had followed his pre-determined path, which would lead him to a dirt field that was next to the embankment, on the side of the I-95 ramp. As he started on the field, he noticed the motorcade just getting to the on-ramp and speeded up. He grabbed the trigger to his vest and headed up the embankment. He hoped he had enough speed to leap over and be over the President's vehicle. He gave it full throttle and rocketed into the air. The last thing he thought about, before pressing the switch, was his family. He wanted them to think of him as a hero.

Mustafa had gone to the rooftop. When he got to the roof entrance, he noticed the door was ajar. He stopped and took out his gun, making sure the silencer was on tight. He peeked out the door and saw a soldier set up on the edge of the roof, with a sniper rifle on a tripod. He lowered his Bass case, which had the RPG and left the case in the stairwell, and slowly went out the door.

He stepped onto the roof and rocks crackled under his foot. The soldier turned around, not expecting anyone to be there, he was not ready. He reached for his side piece, but Mustafa fired five rounds at him, effectively killing him on the spot.

Mustafa checked the man's pulse, and to make sure he was dead, went back, grabbed the RPG, and set it up knowing he had a few minutes to fire. When he saw the lead car getting on the on-ramp, he counted to five and fired. He knew the RPG would not completely damage the President's vehicle but was hoping to cause havoc with what he knew was coming.

He saw a motorcycle leap into the air, and almost explode over the President's motorcade. He waited until the explosions came from under

I-95 and used the dead sniper's rifle, which was all set up. As soon as he saw movement around the vehicles, he started shooting at them. He saw the agent's fire back at him but knew their side arms and automatics would not reach him.

He used the rooftop ledge to stabilize the tripod and fired off some shots, he was patient and fired when he saw movement, and he put in another magazine and saw there were more in the sniper's bag. He saw a shiny reflection off something near the third car, and it was the last thing he saw.

Bahir had the five workers in the back of the van, before he got on the I-95 on-ramp at Forest Hill Boulevard, which was one mile from Southern. He pulled off to the side, took out his gun, and shot all of them dead. They never knew what hit them.

He took off towards Southern, and saw the traffic was already backing up. He took the emergency lane to the entrance to the Southern off-ramp, stopped the van, took a brick from under the seat, placed it on the accelerator, stepped out of the van, reached in and threw it in drive, while jumping to the side. He saw with glee as the van head towards the underpass, before hitting a few cars and causing the van to explode, about the same time the bombs went off the underpass. He thought we could not have timed it better and started running towards the east side of I-95, looking at the embankment about seventy yards in front of him.

He heard shots and explosions and was running up to the edge of the embankment when he grabbed his vest switch. He was making it almost to the top, when he saw a group emerging from the rubble. He yelled "Death to the infidel!" when he was cut down in a hail of automatic fire. I have died a martyr was his last thought.

Fadi and Malik were at the Heliport with their instructor, waiting for the all-clear to go on their Helo training flight. They were standing by the chopper, while it warmed up.

Their instructor was making small talk. "You know, you boys have been exceptional students, perfect grades, perfect attendance. You should not have any problems landing jobs, after you graduate. Where are you boys thinking of applying?"

Malik spoke first. "I'm thinking of going back home, they need good pilots there."

"How about you, Fadi? Where will you go? Are you okay? You look a little nervous, you haven't before."

Fadi stuttered. "I have not given it a lot of thought. I will, soon enough."

Malik had reached into his flight suit, and pulled out a stun gun, and used it on the instructor, who immediately fell on the ground. The boys used tie straps on his legs and arms and jumped in the chopper.

They went thru their checklist, fired it up, and took off. Immediately, there was communication from the flight tower. "Helo one! you are not cleared for take-off, identify yourself!"

Fadi was shaking like a leaf.

"Helo one! I repeat, you are not cleared for takeoff, set the bird down, or you will be fired upon!"

Fadi turned off the comms. "Let's go, let's go!"

Malik turned to Fadi "Got it, my brother, let's make a mark on our enemies."

They headed towards I-95, which was two miles away. Their plan was to crash the chopper into the motorcade, while exploding the bombs in their backpacks.

"Almost there, almost there!" said Malik.

Suddenly, a bullet crashed thru the windshield, barely missing them both.

"Look! Look!" screamed Fadi, pointing at the sky in front of them. They could see a fighter plane heading towards them.

They saw the flare of missile exhaust from under the jet's wings and knew there was no escape.

CHAPTER 51

The ambulance did not head to the emergency room entrance, but to the underground garage. Glen and I looked at each other with a puzzled look.

In the underground garage, there were Sheriff's vehicles, FDLE vehicles, and black SUV's, along with The Tank, and the President's personal ride. The ambulance came to a screeching halt and was surrounded by Secret Service agents. They pulled the EMT from the passenger seat, but before they rushed him into the Tank he turned to us and said "She sure is a fine specimen" and was whisked into the Tank which immediately pulled away, with most of the vehicles following it.

I looked at Glen, Glen looked at me, and we both said: "What the Fuck!" at the same time. The ambulance driver turned, looked at both of us, and laughed. "Very nice to meet you boys. Bill Johnson, President's Secret Service detail."

We were debriefed in the hospital's conference room by Bill Johnson, Susan Schliff, and Sheriff Broadwater.

"We are fortunate to have you boys from the State Attorney's office play golf today, don't know how things would have worked out without you." Bill Johnson was smoking a cigar, even though there were no smoking signs everywhere.

Susan Schliff spoke up. "You know, Castillo, you technically do not work at the State Attorney's office, but we saw where they hired you on occasion, so we'll give you a pass on this one. I'm sure they didn't hire you for your sniper skills."

"No, they hired me for my exemplary deductive skills."

Susan laughed. "You are full of yourself, like your file says. You'll be full of my shoe up your ass if you call me Susie one more time."

Everyone had a good laugh at my expense.

Broadwater pointed at Glen. "West, you and I have worked together for a while, but I would appreciate next time you hire this loose cannon over here to give me a heads up. I looked up his file, and he does not follow protocol, dances to his own tune, and has a vigilante sense of justice."

I couldn't resist. "From hero to villain in just two easy steps, eh Sheriff?

"Just keep your nose clean in Palm Beach County, okay, Castillo?"

"Yes, sir." as I saluted him.

Glen shook his head. "What a jackass!"

"Who, me? or the Sheriff?"

Broadwater left the room in a huff. Johnson and Schliff were trying not to laugh.

"Anything we can do for you, boys? We have you bandaged up, all good?'

"Yes, there is, Bill. Could we get our trophies? We did win it, but POTUS cheated, and took first place from us."

Glen shook his head. "This motherfucker, won't let this go, sorry, Bill."

"I'll see what I can do, thank both of you for your service today, keep it in the short grass."

I got up and stretched, "Let's go have a cocktail and some dinner, brother."

"Sounds good, let's go."

CHAPTER 52

Aaron was taking inventory of what had gone down. It had been a couple of months, and nothing had splashed back to him. The initial investigation had shown that the men had been compared to the 9/11 terrorists. They had blended into society, kept a low profile, and he didn't show on anyone's radar.

Two of the men had been tracked to Yemen, and three to Saudi Arabia. Their funding had been traced to a trading company, which was no longer in business.

Aaron felt safe and was carrying out his duties as Diplomatic Ambassador. He had kept a low profile and had prepared a "Go bag" just in case. When he met with the cell, he would leave his phone in his office, and used only burner phones.

He was disappointed, the mission had failed, but he was proud that an attack of this magnitude was able to be mounted on the infidel's land.

He was meeting with his handler and was told to be ready anytime. He was excited, but leery at the same time. He had been given a ticket for a skybox at the Florida Panthers hockey arena, so he headed there.

Upon arrival at the skybox, the only person there was his handler. "Hello, Alec. Just you and I are here?"

They shook hands, and Aaron was always impressed with the colorful outfits Alec wore. He certainly wanted to stand out, which explained why his hair was jelled, and standing straight up was much like Guy Fieri's.

"Aaron, good to see you again. So sorry our event did not have the outcome we desired, even though we double crossed those boys into thinking it was for their cause, when it was really for our cause."

"I know, but it was a hell of a try."

"Indeed. Grab a drink, and let's chat about the upcoming Diplomatic State dinner you will be attending." Alec pointed towards the bar.

So, there it was, Aaron thought, they knew his schedule and wondered if they wanted him to turn someone or wanted someone compromised for a future favor or two.

Alex switched to Russian. "If you don't mind, let's speak in our native tongue, even though I have a sound cancellation device that I brought with me, one can never be too careful."

Aaron easily switched to Russian, he was starting to think there was more to this than turning a double agent.

They grabbed drinks, and sat in the middle of the room, away from the entrance door and the seats in front.

Alex cleared his throat. "I will get right to it. I will be handing you a small container with Novichok, the nerve agent, used on the Skripal's in London. You will take it with you to the State dinner, and if you have an opportunity, "Number one" will be there, if you get a chance, use it. It will be almost impossible to put it in his beverage due to his security detail. I have a suggestion that will require the ultimate sacrifice on your part, it is in a powder form. If you put some on your hand when you shake hands with him, it will be easy to infect him. Of course, you will be infected too, but I promise we will whisk you out of the country and get you home for treatment with Atropine as soon as possible. I know it is a lot to take in, but take your time, and ask any questions you might have."

Aaron's heart was racing, and he was momentarily stunned with what was proposed to him. He took a deep breath, and a healthy swig of his drink. "Wow, I...I need a moment to think."

"But of course, of course my comrade. Let's take in a bit of the game, both goalies are Russians, we certainly train the best goalies in hockey, cheers, my friend."

CHAPTER 53

Jose had finished the GTX and was happy how it turned out. The road test was good, and everything worked to his liking. His client, "Jimmy the K" was coming to pick it up in a few hours, and he could use the payment for his services. The car had turned out very nice.

It was known as the Miami Vice GTX which was featured in the premier episode of that show. It was manufactured in October of 1967 which made it a 1968. Plymouth only produced 1,026 convertibles for that year's model.

For the gearheads it came with the 440 Commando engine creating 375 horsepower. This one came with a four-speed transmission and a 3.54 Dana sure grip rear-end. The owner garage kept it of course and drove it about once a month with the top down, only way to drive that baby.

Jose heard the front door open and, without looking figured it was either Gafford or Nate, since Kat was still out of town on a photo shoot.

Jose turned around and saw Nate holding a box.

"Hey, Brother, found this by the front door, it's from the White House, you sure it's safe to open? Could be a bomb."

"I'm not expecting anything from them. Why don't you open it, and find out?"

"Maybe it's your Presidential Medal of Honor, for what you did for the President."

"Shit my man, not even a peep out if him, and not even a thank you or a Presidential coaster."

"Well, maybe he saw your postings on social media about him. Open it up, I'm curious!"

Jose opened the box, took out the Styrofoam, and pulled out a trophy with *"First Place, Little Smiles Golf Tournament"* engraved on it.

Nate and Jose laughed.

"I'll be damned, finally got it, we did deserve it."

"POTUS has a sense of humor, after all." Nate slapped Jose on the back. "At least, you won't be crying about it anymore."

"You know about me and justice, it just rubbed me the wrong way he had to cheat to win his own tournament. By the way, what brings you to my humble abode?"

"I was just tracking a lead in the area and figured I'd drop in. I appreciate the info Gafford got for me on the phone logs of the victims of our serial killer. We are putting together a list of suspects, but you know the short staffing have affected our personnel, so it is going slow. It's hard to do surveillance on multiple suspects, which is where you come in."

"Ah, I wondered when you were going to get to the point."

"I just wanted to let you know that, once we whittle the list down to a manageable number of suspects, I would like to use you on a consulting basis to help out, unofficially of course."

"Of course, buddy, I will be happy to help. You get the list to me once you get it, and I will be more than happy to assist."

"I would appreciate it, this guy has bewildered us, no DNA left at the crime scenes, not a speck of evidence. This guy manages to get in without forcible entry, and he has all the time in the world to carry his plan out. How he manages to cross into these women's life is diabolic."

I had no idea helping Nate out would bring me to protect the one I love the most.

CHAPTER 54

I had made an appointment to see Pushkin trying to figure out a way, letting him know that I knew what they were up to. We met at Joe's Stone Crab on Washington Avenue in Miami Beach. It was busy for lunch, stone crab season was almost over, so people were trying to get their fix in, before those delicacies were all gone.

I was there so often, that I had made friends with Sergio, the Maître' D, and getting a table for two was not a problem. I ordered a gin and tonic, with Bombay Sapphire, extra lime, and waited for Pushkin to show.

A few minutes later, there was a wall of large men by the entrance, and I saw Sergio bringing Pushkin to the table. His bodyguards worked their way to the bar and took seats where they could watch our table.

Pushkin sat down, and looked at the table setting to make sure everything was in its proper place. I noticed he was wearing a *Guayabera* shirt with cotton slacks. He ordered a Lychee Martini.

"I see you have found much a cooler outfit to wear, nice choice on the shirt."

"Yes, I took your advice. The wardrobe I brought from Europe is way too heavy for South Florida."

"Indeed, it was, glad to see you are acclimating, if you think it is bad, wait till August and September. I took the liberty to order stone crabs for the both of us, it is a must if you come to Joe's."

"Thank you, I have heard of Joe's, it looks very classy, and the crowd says it all. I am curious as to our meeting, so please do ask what you are concerned about."

"I wanted to let you know I was doing a job for the Indian casino, and as a result it appears that there might be some interest from your associates in, as we say in the States "worming" their way into the casino." I did the air quote, couldn't resist.

Alec took a sip of his martini, and his smile reminded me of a weasel. "There is no harm in adopting the American way of capitalism, the Globalization of economies has changed the world as we once knew it. If you do not change and adapt, you will fall behind."

"Agreed, Alec, but it is dangerous to mix aggressive expansion with heavy handed ways of the past. I have been contracted by the casino to look into any improprieties, such as the bombing of an apartment in Tampa, belonging to a couple that worked at the casino and had some ancillary activities, due to their familial connections."

"Well, Jose, I assure you that, even though we are aggressively expanding our business models, we will do everything we can to keep things above board, but I have no knowledge of the Tampa situation."

The Stone crabs were brought to our table. I decided to get my point across, before starting to eat.

"Let's just say I do not have any proof of your organization's involvement in Tampa at this time, but if I do find in the future that there was and I find the involvement is anything I consider illegal, I will be your worst enemy."

Alec drank some of his martini, placed it carefully in front of him, buying some time clearly measuring his words. "Dear Jose, the animus you hold towards our group is well known. We respect your dedication to what you believe are the scales of justice, regardless of whether you place your hand on the scale to tip it. Just make sure you can live with your decisions regarding your actions against us, because actions can bring consequences."

"Got it, loud and clear, just remember consequences work both ways, let's enjoy our lunch, and trust that in the future we may have disagreements. But I, on my end, will try to bring a reasonable and logical conclusion to those differences."

Alec picked up his glass "*Na Zdorvie!* May we live to be old men."

Jose picked up his cocktail. "*Salud*, agreed, may we all." Jose had a feeling that, at some point, he would hold Alec's life in his hands, and he would have no compunction at all, no hesitation, and no guilt doing what he thought was needed.

EPILOGUE

David woke up and felt fantastic. He went over in his head the night he spent with Monica and was very pleased with himself. He had burned everything he had worn and started planning to do some shopping to replace the items he had burned.

He started thinking about which of his customers he would target next and thought about that cute blonde with the Southern accent that drove a BMW. Just thinking about it gave him a hard-on. She had mentioned that she was out of town often so he checked off in his head that once he did the deed she wouldn't be missed for a few days or longer.

He had a special feeling about this one and could not wait to get started on his next project.

Don't miss out!

Visit the website below and you can sign up to receive emails whenever Jorge Goyanes publishes a new book. There's no charge and no obligation.

https://books2read.com/r/B-A-KQIY-DVWHG

BOOKS 2 READ

Connecting independent readers to independent writers.